THE STONE DOOR

LEONORA CARRINGTON (1917–2011) was born in Lancashire, England, to an industrialist father and an Irish mother. She was raised on fantastical folktales told to her by her Irish nanny at her family's estate, Crookhey Hall. Carrington would be expelled from two convent schools before enrolling in art school in Florence. In 1937, a year after her mother gave her a book on surrealist art featuring Max Ernst's work, she met the artist at a party. Not long after, Carrington and the then-married Ernst settled in the south of France, where Carrington completed her first major painting, *Self-Portrait (The Inn of the Dawn Horse)*, in 1938. In the wake of Ernst's imprisonment by the Nazis, Carrington fled to Spain, where she suffered a nervous breakdown and was committed to a mental hospital in Santander. She eventually escaped to the Mexican embassy in Lisbon and settled first in New York and later in Mexico, where she married the photographer Imre "Chiki" Weisz and had two sons. Carrington spent much of the rest of her life in Mexico City, moving in a circle of like-minded artists that included Remedios Varo and Alejandro Jodorowsky. Among Carrington's published works are the novels *The Hearing Trumpet* and *The Stone Door*; two collections of short stories; and a memoir of madness, *Down Below*. *The Hearing Trumpet*, *Down Below*, and *The Milk of Dreams*, an illustrated group of stories she originally wrote for her children, are also available from New York Review Books.

GABRIEL WEISZ CARRINGTON is a writer and has published poetry, essays, and other works of literature and theater around the world. He teaches classes in literature and theater at the National

Autonomous University of Mexico and is president of the Fundación Leonora Carrington A.C. (Leonora Carrington Foundation) in collaboration with Daniel Weisz Argomedo and Martha Patricia Argomedo Manrique.

ANNA WATZ is an associate professor of English literature at Uppsala University, Sweden. She is the author of *Angela Carter and Surrealism: "A Feminist Libertarian Aesthetic"* and the editor of *A History of the Surrealist Novel* and *Surrealist Women's Writing: A Critical Exploration*.

THE STONE DOOR

LEONORA CARRINGTON

Introduction by
GABRIEL WEISZ CARRINGTON

Afterword by
ANNA WATZ

NEW YORK REVIEW BOOKS

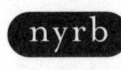

New York

THIS IS A NEW YORK REVIEW BOOK
PUBLISHED BY THE NEW YORK REVIEW OF BOOKS
207 East 32nd Street, New York, NY 10016
www.nyrb.com

Originally published in French translation as *La Porte de pierre*.
First published as an NYRB Classic in 2025.

An earlier version of the afterword by Anna Watz, entitled "'A Language Buried at the Back of Time': *The Stone Door* and Poststructuralist Feminism," was published in *Leonora Carrington and the International Avant-Garde*, edited by Jonathan P. Eburne and Catriona McAra (Manchester University Press, 2017).

Library of Congress Cataloging-in-Publication Data
Names: Carrington, Leonora, 1917–2011, author.
Title: The stone door / by Leonora Carrington; Introduction by Gabriel Weisz Carrington, afterword by Anna Watz.
Description: New York: New York Review Books, 2025. | Series: New York Review Books classics
Identifiers: LCCN 2024008771 (print) | LCCN 2024008772 (ebook) | ISBN 9781681378947 (paperback) | ISBN 9781681378954 (e-book)
Subjects: LCGFT: Fantasy fiction. | Novels.
Classification: LCC PR6053.A6965 S76 2024 (print) | LCC PR6053.A6965 (ebook) | DDC 823/.914—dc23/eng/20240221
LC record available at https://lccn.loc.gov/2024008771
LC ebook record available at https://lccn.loc.gov/20

ISBN 978-1-68137-894-7
Available as an electronic book; ISBN 978-1-68137-895-4

The authorized representative in the EU for product safety and compliance is eucomply OÜ, Pärnu mnt 139b-14, 11317 Tallinn, Estonia, hello@eucompliancepartner.com, +33 757690241.

Printed in the United States of America on acid-free paper.
10 9 8 7 6 5 4 3 2

CONTENTS

Introduction · vii

THE STONE DOOR · 1

Afterword · 113

INTRODUCTION
Numinous Door!

THE FIRST lines lead to the sanctum of a black forest, likened to the black hair of an Aztec priest. These are the connections of the marvelous. The sentences continue, a manor house is tortoiseshell, a dragon's hide. *You explain that the architecture conveys the sadness of the neo-Gothic.* A manic mixture of architectural styles. The house of your memories is humid, assailed by fungi, green and orange. The remembered household decays. Characters are compared to the materiality of rocks. In an observatory three wondrous figures appear—a "Chinaman," a European, and a Jew—one is gazing at the moon, another looking through a microscope, the third is examining a flower. The Chinaman feels intellectually superior to women. He is afraid of sharing a secret with females, and he declares, "No woman must ever learn more than the circle around her hearth." *Who are the three sages? Did you ever meet them in your dreamland? Were these personifications of wisdom manifestations of a personal inner wisdom?*

There is a door to female knowledge, they concur—the door of the womb—which represents a threat to male ability. This introduces a gendered politics into the magical realm. The section ends like a theater performance: The lights dim, the men disappear. A new archetypical metaphor emerges as a house resembling a pyramid appears, in contrast to the manor. These structures reoccur intermittently throughout the text as references to Mexico and England.

Buildings and characters are malleable in the mind of the writer. Houses themselves are organic entities. "'The house has grown,' said the green-eyed man." *You inhabit an imaginary architecture assembled by your mind, you are back at Crookhey Hall or Hazelwood, where you lived in your youth. A series of sensations embraces your subtle body. Through this you explore foundational themes, returning to the Victorian abode as a way of becoming those places; these have a mnemonic quality; habitations allow a nostalgic return to England. Similarly, you take us to Hungary, to your husband Chiki's birthplace. These scenes draw upon the reality of the concentration camp, the terrible experience of losing one's identity, of becoming a mere number.* Enchanted dominions are gateways to the unseen. The narrative connects the supernatural to emotional upheaval, and the characters enter a magical world with a mission to fulfill.

The character Amagoya is haunted by "ancestral horses from the British Isles." These animals recall the horses of Leonora's youth in England. *The Stone Door* is an emotional, marvel-related biography. Some of Amagoya's feelings echo Leonora's; the author will use her for cathartic release, projecting emotions onto her.

"Words are treacherous because they are incomplete. The written word hangs in time like a lump of lead." But words are also powerful. After an invocation, the narrator predicts that "In some mysterious way these words will enter life." A few paragraphs later, she discovers the stone door, which she is unable to open.

Leonora's world teems with such magical devices: the ivory box or the enchanted circle. Animals, among them cats and ponies, abound. Amagoya hears a voice singing "Llorona." *This legendary Aztec woman mourns the children she has drowned; her fate is to seek her offspring through rivers, towns, and cities. A favorite figure of yours, she has always puzzled you.* These figures of Llorona and the horses represent the emotional touchstones of England and Mexico.

The uncanny soon intrudes into the unnamed narrator's world: "a stranger bringing in the New Year" arrives. The narrator contemplates putting on a wolfskin and howling at the moon. *You perform your anguish and become a furred creature. You quench your distress with these miraculous transformations. This text is an emotional biography, quite eloquent.* "Yet I dare not go. Return, ghost, animal or man. I cannot bear this loneliness. I am sick of being alone with myself." We have entered a story that heals loneliness by giving voice to emotional states. The narrator puts on a wolf mask and comes eye to eye with a wolf, discovers that the wolf hides behind himself as she hides from herself. Magical transformations reveal hidden realms within oneself.

The narrator sniffs an ivory box and is assailed by memories. As readers we too will experience intense scents, images, sounds, and flavors; we participate in the secret body of the novel and feel the text. The narrator lapses into a hypnagogic state, dreaming a journey through Mesopotamia to Hungary. Along the way she finds tombs resembling tropical fish. She travels to the land of the dead, bringing a toy for the Lord Mayor of Bagdad from the King of the Jews. The dream state weaves stories out of objects, places, animals, foods.

The world of *The Stone Door* is an unstable one, where everything is prone to radical alternation. Shape-shifters abound, limbs disappear. Mirrors play an important role, announcing transformation. Amagoya observes herself in the mirror and discovers that her nude reflection resembles an ivory mannequin. The next moment, she finds in it a resemblance to a black dog. It is not long before an actual ivory doll appears. In this way, aleatory affinities are made real. There is a thread connecting Amagoya to the ivory doll. Seeking explanation, Amagoya will encounter the Artisan, an older woman, a doll maker; she is the archetypical artist Leonora carries in her mental underworld. The artisan is associated with the crone and with ancient female wisdom. Her prophetic voice announces, "Mercury speaks to Ivory; hear me, I am the Artisan but I am also Mercury." She performs an alchemical procedure that turns the inanimate ivory into two living homunculi. She throws these figures into the fire; I wonder if, like the phoenix, they are reborn. This is the alchemical story of transmutation, the nature of things returning to a mercurial first matter.

Leonora's family, myself included, usually ate meals in the kitchen. Here Leonora invented strange dishes for friends as well. This wild spirit of experimentation finds its way into *The Stone Door*: "'I am going to add a few fried plums and raisins,' said Phillip stirring the mixture" early in the book. *How is it that you prepare the amorphous materials for a sketch, a drawing, a painting, or the unknown projection of a spectral body? Yet the character of Phillip is not a particular male from your past but a means of dialogue with maleness.* Many pages later, Phillip cooks a dragon, *and thus you blend a homely kitchen scene with a dream. A symbolic story takes shape, bleeding from the visual realm into the narrative one.* We encounter another dragon, this one black, living among documents. A faceless man kills the creature, and it, too, goes into the stew.

We follow Zacharias, also known as 105, to the carnival. A wax woman lies on a silk bed; a demon, a dwarf, a monkey, and a serpent complete the tableau. *You direct the audience's gaze to the iconography of horror.* Deformed syphilitic people assail the young man. The scene grows more horrific: "a thing which looked like a monster sewing machine with a needle as long as a man's body and stained with clots of blood." *You summon, as well, a little girl who has grown up in England as Zacharias has in Hungary. These emotional points coexist in your mind.* The setting shifts rapidly to a ritual space. A ram emerges from a pond; it is a sacrificial animal. *You change the tone of your narrative as you now move into a numinous domain. And this is where you feel your way into Zacharias's pent-up emotions. He is a victim of an authoritarian rule that destroys feeling in order to "educate" individuals into the ways of the patriarchy.* Zacharias, in this context, is a personification of intuitive knowledge. Along this journey inward, Leonora also brings in Mexican mythology, a touchstone for her own travels into the ancient recesses of the mind.

The symbol of the egg holds particular meaning in her world, and in *The Stone Door* we are shown a scene of oomancy, or divination by egg. We might recall the section of Leonora's one-time partner Max Ernst's invented biography, in which he claims that he "came out of the egg which his mother had laid in an eagle's nest and which the bird had brooded for seven years." For both artists, the egg serves as an athanor, or alchemical oven. "The Egg trembled very slightly, without communicating any meaning to me. I then understood that the word to address such a primitive and embryonic body would have to come from a language buried at the back of time," writes Leonora in *The Stone Door*. In their work Leonora and Max fashioned archetypical companions for themselves—for Leonora, the horse, and for Ernst, Loplop, Father Superior of Birds.

According to Jung, "'infantile' or unconscious forces [may be] represented as Cabiri and hobgoblins." Such might be the source of Zacharias's "white child" persona. However, we must caution against a fully Jungian reading of this novel, since we cannot know for sure if Leonora consulted Jung in its writing. It is more fruitful to approach her work as a mythical imaginary construct all her own. She created a unique symbology, a complex bricolage where imagination and creative persona entwine. At various times, Zacharias is associated with mythic entities like the white child of Mesopotamia, the wise King, the Jew, or the sacrificial ram. Zacharias is "haggard and dirty, his clothes jagged and torn, a mixture between a young scarecrow and the crows it was supposed to scare." He is a liminal figure, encompassing two things simultaneously, a complete range of identities.

Zacharias finds work with the Chinaman, now identified as Chung Ming Lo. *As I come upon the Chinaman, I recall your painting* Habdalah Asejaledha *(1959), where you depict Chinese men tending horses, the humorous and playful understanding of your imaginary theater.* Ming Lo is the maker of all manner of astonishing objects. In his workshop we find a magic mirror, a means of becoming acquainted with one's face and, of course, with the whole range of one's identity. Here Zacharias discovers and steals a stone key. Ming Lo sends him on a journey, and on the train he meets a stranger lacking facial features; one wonders if this indeterminate appearance is representative of the lack of identity we often feel in dreams. The stranger knows of the door. We learn that doors might be accessible—or prohibited—and that a door acts as protection from all that threatens from without.

Zacharias steps into an enchanted threshold where the mirror and the door meet. Rituals invoking guardians or spirits take place here: "One of those silent nights, when the snow fell outside, you looked deeply into your steel mirror and your image said: 'I hear.' Let me in, let me in, Stone Door." Zacharias discovers "the enormous corpse of a bearded king," who presently has shrunk "to the dimensions of a newborn babe." Through alchemy, this corpse returns to its original size. From the remaining skin, Zacharias will fashion a pair of trousers fit for a giant. Giants belong to the fabulous world of fairy tales and childish nightmares. They are associated with monstrous emotion; they are the personification of otherness. And yet, these shadow selves can often turn out to be helpers.

At first, Zacharias cannot open the door, even with the help of the stone key. He pleads to gain access, and a woman's voice answers, "Break through it with words, blows, prayers, or music." Zacharias fulfills his quest only once he crosses the magical threshold of the stone door and unites with the symbolic woman. It is true that the door might appear inaccessible, and yet through magical means it will open and lead one to another reality.

—Gabriel Weisz Carrington

THE STONE DOOR

I

IN THE middle of a deep forest, black and alive as an Aztec sacerdote's hair, stood a big house. Victorian style, very sad neo-Gothic, Grecian, a Roman corner here and there as if the architect had wrought a terrible revenge on his school days. This great building was incongruously crowned with a tower which was really an observatory.

When it rained, humidity pressed around the house and clung to the walls till a crop of fungi varying from green to orange, speckled sepia to purple covered the walls giving a colored hide like that of a dragon. Even the prancing centaur on top of the observatory had a pelt of wild mushrooms; this made him look as if he was made of felt, not stone.

The three men who sat silently in the observatory under the centaur were watching the moon which was well on the wane. They were dressed in clean white linen and sat at equal distances around a table. Each man had a telescope, a microscope and a flower which they examined meticulously, now and again jotting down a figure in chalk on the black table.

The oldest of the three men, who appeared to be of Asiatic origin, possibly from China, sat as if hewn to the chair, his hands lying before him like trained dogs. His eyes had not quit the waning moon for twelve hours.

The second man, a European, with heavy reddish flesh and light eyes, fidgeted with his microscope and made busy signs on the table which he rubbed out more often than not. Occasionally he moved his round head in jerks or stirred his feet under the table.

The third and youngest of the three men was a Jew. He had a pale handsome face and warm eyes. The white linen robe he wore seemed a part of his person and became him well. His right hand traced a slow caress on the palm of his left hand and he watched this with evident pleasure.

He has ceased looking at the moon.

The Chinaman suddenly moved and the shock stilled the other two men.

From his white garment he drew a piece of knotted string and dangled it before their eyes. The string seemed to writhe in his fingers.

The European arose rather clumsily, having contemplated the string, and fetched three earthenware pots which had been waiting in readiness on a small table near the door. One of these pots contained water, the other wine, the last new milk.

The water he set before the Chinaman, the wine before his own empty seat, and the milk was for the Jew.

Somewhere in the great house a bell tolled and this broke the long silence.

"No," said the Jew. "It will not do any more."

The European looked shocked and shifted his feet. The Chinaman did not move.

"The milk," continued the Jew, caressing his hands. "If I suck all the cows in Europe dry, we will not know any more."

"We have seen war," said the European. "Famine in Europe and uncountable bodies violently killed."

"Unfortunately," replied the Chinaman, "the necessity for that is written in the arched parchment over our heads."

"To what end?" asked the European. "The treasure of the last war went into Hipolita's maw."

"The powers are knotted; they must break loose," said the Chinaman.

"Drink your milk," the European told the Jew angrily, "perhaps it can still mend."

"No, I am running dry; I must have a woman."

They saw him clearly for the first time and were horrified at the sight. He continued to caress the palm of his left hand.

"If we ignore the door of the womb we shall shrivel and die."

"The danger of sharing such a secret," said the Chinaman eventually, "would loosen all the damning powers in the Universe. No woman must ever learn more than the circle around her hearth."

The Jew did not appear to be listening. "Sweet chaos," he murmured to himself, "and out of that chaos a new chaotic order never before dreamed by man."

A black dog, wringing wet, pushed open the door and ran to the Chinaman.

"We will go downstairs and smoke, it is time to dissolve."

The light faded and the men and the observatory disappeared in darkness.

2

WHEN THE knocking came at last, Amagoya did not go to the door at once. She waited a few seconds, twisting her fingers.

They had left seven months before and now for five weeks she had waited for the knocking. It came as an anticlimax.

To get to the house they had to enter a twisted brick passage like a pyramid. Amagoya had time to imagine them standing outside, the fat woman and the fat green-eyed man.

When she opened the door, they repeated the picture in her head, smiling and uneasy, dressed in the same clothes, saying the same words. They kissed all around: people hiding something.

"The house has grown," said the green-eyed man.

"Very soon they'll ask me," thought Amagoya, smiling.

The fat woman walked through the kitchen staring about her curiously.

A pink flannel curtain in the doorway moved slightly.

"This side is perfectly symmetrical to the other," said the fat woman.

"She still hates her," thought Amagoya.

They passed through the pink curtain and entered the room in silence. Amagoya had a nervous desire to laugh, as if in the presence of the dead.

The man was quiet and uneasy because something seemed

to move in the room apart from themselves. Looking about he noticed with some relief that the door opening onto a small patio had rickety hinges and draughts blew through, making small restless noises.

"She doesn't live here now," said Amagoya in a flat voice. "She went away."

They heard somebody come in and walk about in the other room.

"Amagoya..." called a man's voice. "They haven't finished yet. One could expect such a thing in this devil-ridden bird's nest of a town...."

"They are here," replied Amagoya. "Wenceslaus, Phillip and... Michelle have arrived...."

A white-haired man pushed through the curtain.

Greetings were carefully exchanged all over again, with less kissing. Wenceslaus and Phillip went out together, leaving Amagoya alone with the fat woman.

"Is she happy now?" asked Michelle, sitting down on the bed.

"I think so," said Amagoya carefully.

"Still I thought she would stay with Pedro forever." The fat woman lit a cigarette.

"I cannot help thinking that she is more superficial than we had imagined."

"How she must hate her..." thought Amagoya.

"Phillip confided some very important knowledge to her and I sometimes wonder if he made a mistake."

"I must try and remember all this," thought Amagoya.

"After all," continued Michelle, "how could one know? She possessed such sagacity on subjects that take many more years than hers to learn."

"When you both went away everything changed," said

Amagoya. "Nobody thought you would ever come back. Nothing seems very stable at this height, I think people become strange and do things they would not think of doing at sea level."

"Ah, the altitude . . ." exclaimed Michelle. "The altitude is terrible. . . . Tell me, Amagoya, when did she leave you?"

"On New Year's Eve, on the stroke of midnight."

Amagoya noticed that she was sniffing the air, holding the cigarette from her face.

"She was always busy."

"Is that a bird singing? What a sharp voice!"

"We call him Don Mazarino. One morning a bright red bird flew into my room. We never knew how he got in as all the doors and windows were closed. He's a cardinal. He appeared just a short time after you went away."

"He's like a clot of blood. . . . What does he eat?" Michelle poked a bit of banana at the red bird and laughed at his fear.

"Yes," said Amagoya, "he has a sharp voice, like a whip."

An empty tin on the table had burst unaccountably into flame, and Michelle was not listening. She got up, her mouth hard in the soft round face. Deliberately she quenched the flame and sat down.

"She was a very clever girl. . . ."

When they had gone Amagoya went back into the room alone. For a time she thought about the two fat people and why they had returned. They always had hated the lofty city and hating they had expected the secrets to climb out of tombs and pyramids to make themselves known. Perhaps hate as well as love could reveal secrets.

Amagoya was conscious once again of the absence in the

room. A legion of ancestral horses from the British Isles had swum the grey Atlantic to haunt her wherever she went. New Year's Eve came back into her mind like the ticking of a clock one tried not to hear.

The little doctor had called her "Witch-ridden, haunted ... a jade who passed her nights hob-nobbing with banshees...." He had died since.

They were sitting in the room near the bar with the lights out, somebody was chanting the song of the Llorona.

Midnight had tolled and the door opened to a stranger bringing in the New Year. She shrieked and held out her hands which he took and held for a long time.

Amagoya shuddered. That night a dead Spaniard in the bar; the Norwegian Giant who sat in the fire. How she had blasphemed and vomited into the geraniums outside the front door.

To push the thoughts away, Amagoya rummaged amongst the papers which lay as if forgotten in a black tin trunk. The small neat writing covered pages in order.

September 15th. Cancer. Illness, New York. Cancer. Tropic of (Mexico). Cancer, fourth place in the circle. Water Father. Spider-Crab. Mizte-cacihautl's box, (*6*) Scorpion-crab for funeral paraphernalia. Tiger-spider-crab in dream.

Night. I am confused. Not only is the word gross and stupid, it lies by what it leaves unsaid. Why the Hell won't the two of you leave me alone?

You imagine you are looking for the Truth, Michelle? Believe me, you breed lies like microbes but worse you bore me . . . and your body, your fat stale body revolts me. Moreover I pity you, and what a tasteless grey food is pity!

The star follows her strange course in the mountains, in the round temples, through green, lukewarm woods and penetrating hedges and walls. She lies hard, bright and cold under the beds of lovers or under bodies of sleeping cattle.

I never cease spying on the star's course.

Let me have revenge. You know I am tender: craters of honey which can't be freed till I can use all the arms of hate.

Father, let me torture little children. I want to persecute them, Father, with a frank and humble smile. Teach me to be a hypocrite. Then, Father, what a lover I shall be.

(After some hour's pause, it is later than midnight)

Pedro came in drunk again, I made him a screeching sordid scene and yet I am stuck like a rat in a trap. Will I ever be free? What secret craving keeps me near him?

I think about Phillip.

Day. The cuckoo clock is driving me wild. I am always alone, that is what makes me suffer. Damn that bird.

Words are treacherous because they are incomplete. The written word hangs in time like a lump of lead. Everything should move with the ages and the planets.

The trap outside the circle. Calculate the way out. Pentagonal crown on Virgo, death impregnated with life. I have learned to stop laughing by wrapping my face in the tripeless corpse of a dog. Howling at the moon has its charms; the moon throws shadows in reply. I howl at the moon for the rest of my days.

The time has come for the star to appear once more.

Perhaps I will dress in wolfskin, sitting in a tree watching the circle, waiting for the next step to be traced in the mud.

Sometimes I think that I am alone and I shriek with misery and rage.

Horse and Hattock and go.

All these shadows from the unknown. I am ignorant, but soon I shall begin to know.

September 18th. I played a game with Amagoya. (How much, I wonder, does she know?)

Late October evening. Nothing ever prevents me from rushing home after six o'clock. We know only too well that Pedro won't be there. Leaving Amagoya I run down Calle Moreno straining my eyes to see if there is a light in my window. Black, black as hearses. This never ceases to twist my guts.

The same old thing yesterday only I didn't wait alone and tortured in the empty apartment. (I shall never know anything until I am free of this.) Walking about alone in the streets, Amagoya would be afraid. As I walked I found that I had evoked someone and felt sure that it was Phillip, remembering that he had said how dangerous it is to evoke live people. (Dangerous for whom?) Then I thought that he might really be somewhere near hurrying along looking like a round planet in a Burberry. No known person appeared, however, and I realized against my will that the creature evoked was not Phillip, nor anything I could remember. But the presence was reminiscent of something well known.

I am disappointed for I would have liked to evoke Phillip.

When I was a child I wanted to dream of my Shetland pony, who was always too fat to gallop. Black Bess, I wanted to dream of her galloping ahead of my grandfather's Flying Fox, who never lost a race.

But when Nannie turned out the lights, think as I would of Bessie winning the Grand National, Tomie—the game keeper's eight-toed cat—entered my dreams uninvited, stalking through the night at my side. What creature then, uninvited like Tomie the eight-toed cat, came on my walk? Animal or human? Bird, mineral, vegetable or fish? Dark and warm, smelling of dust and cinnamon.

I must find out who it was, but how?

It is still October. A clue, October, the scales. The man and woman in the egg. The house of the Sleeping Winds. They hang together like witchstones made into a broken necklace. Clues because they smell of the same sensation, how or why I cannot say.

The ivory box lined with sandalwood which I used to sniff when nobody was in the drawing room. The ivory box awakened unnamed memories.

Today Michelle showed me the first and basic numbers with their meanings. She said Phillip was angry that she had done this without asking his permission. He was very angry and had threatened to show us no more of the circle. All that is secret and one risks death for disclosing the things he told us. How can anyone be "Shown" if they do not already know? A color cannot be shown or explained to a blind man.

Phillip tells Michelle everything like a little boy. After we went to see Coatlique, mother of Huitzilopochtli, she made a scene. She says I am a devil. When I met Phillip secretly at the owl, she already knew. Quetzalcoatl—river, water, father-mother. Phillip thinks there will be important events here. The Gods are malevolent and dangerous. He is afraid.

The sign will appear and we shall See and Know. This is what he says.

Somehow I think it is like looking for one's left hand a thousand miles away from one's body.

Yet I am learning to read letters that never appeared in my known alphabet.

The last days of October. Divination is difficult with isolated incidents. Weaving them together into prophecy is an arduous labor which demands constant vigilance. Hazard is a word dropped out of the unknown. Several hazards sometimes make a whole sentence. My memory twitches into a sharp image of something never seen, yet remembered and so acutely alive that I am possessed.

A pine forest white with snow in a country where the people are dressed in bright colors. A noise of smashed glass. Little ragged horses as swift and powerful as tigers. Snow, dust and cinnamon.

Wearing a mask I am on all fours with my nose almost touching the nose of a wolf. Our eyes united in a look, yet I remain hidden behind myself and the wolf hidden behind himself; we are divided by our separate bodies. However deeply we look into each other's eyes a transparent wall divides us from explosion where the looks cross outside our bodies. If by some sage power I could capture that explosion, that mysterious area outside where the wolf and I are one, perhaps then the first door would open and reveal the chamber beyond.

Last night in a dream It returned. A creature wearing a

shaggy skin and smelling of dust and cinnamon. Screaming, I entered the fur, wool or hair, crying tears that were dark and sticky like blood. Tears thick with centuries of agony remembered all at once, they matted the furry coat and stank of birth and death. Shamelessly abandoning all that anguish to this man, animal, vegetable or demon. Then I was in entire possession of the five sensorial powers and their long roots were as visible as the sun. The light of a vision or a dream is united to any given luminous body outside. No longer alone in my own body.

Thoughts and dreams but not a particle of dust to prove their reality. Meanwhile I am wasting each living day in captivity.

All Saints Day. Phillip and Michelle are returning to the Tropics. It is unbearable to imagine that life will step back to the dreary round of scenes with Pedro and escape with Amagoya. Phillip has made me miserable and leaves me alone when my arms are just beginning to feather. Alone I must work myself free and penetrate what mysteries I can. Obviously this captivity stilts whatever knowledge I may possess. What will become of me? I feel like a child left alone with a monster steam engine as a play thing. Which screw must I turn first?

Yesterday I spoke with Phillip of what I have understood. I did not, however, mention the dark creature although I attempted to learn more about him. As always, he answered the questions: "Objects contain the past, present and future, if we know how to trap their secrets." Perhaps a mirror never loses an image once reflected in its surface. Such images can appear again.

Sorcerers and alchemists knew about animal, vegetable and mineral bodies. To hack away the crust of what we have forgotten and rediscover things we knew before we were born.

November 16th. They were gone.

Strangely enough I do not miss them as I had imagined.

The day they left I rode a white horse through the woods of Chapultepec. A grey early morning and few people were about. I galloped around the Palace thinking all the while of my loneliness and of the creature dressed in wool and smelling of cinnamon and dust. Try as I would I could not evoke his real presence and he remained a thought. The formula for this evocation is somewhere hidden inside of me, I feel small and ignorant and this pleases me not at all. I cannot accept this, I want to feel enormous and powerful. (I secretly believe that I am a goddess with very short moments of incarnation.) At the moment Pedro and I loathe each other. We scream ourselves to sleep like fish wives. This is a terrible waste of good energy. Yet I dare not go. Return, ghost, animal or man. I cannot bear this loneliness, I am sick of being alone with myself.

November 20th. I have questioned Amagoya but she can tell me nothing. Of course I cannot tell her exactly what happened with Phillip. Several nights ago I was alone, Pedro being absent as usual. Making a cup of coffee I resolved to be firmly indifferent to his neglect. It is difficult not to feel like an abandoned kitchen maid. Drinking my coffee in my dreary little hole of a kitchen, I pondered about myself.

"I am sitting here alone. I am a fool, a person letting

herself starve to death because the odor of food is usually more exquisite than its taste. No philosopher ever told me if one could catch up in taste the aroma of roasting coffee."

While I was busy telling myself this, in a futile attempt to shut out my loneliness, a small white packet on the table caught my eye. Undoing it curiously I found several sticks of cinnamon. I did not remember having bought cinnamon that day.

Cheered, yet afraid, I took myself to bed and placed the cinnamon under my pillow, to give any passing succubus a sporting chance.

When I closed my eyes the following dream, memory or vision unrolled: I was crossing Mesopotamia on foot and carried a load on my back. It is difficult to say if the load was heavy or light because I already seemed to be accustomed to carrying loads and this had become a function of my body.

My destination was Hungary, which apparently shared a frontier with Mesopotamia. The country in which I travelled was barren, with hardly a tree to be seen. The dusty waste was interrupted here and there by tombs of all shapes and sizes, beautifully decorated and painted like a tropical fish. Looking around me I noticed that the people were not entirely human but on the contrary were partially of clay. They glided slowly through the dust, now and then colliding and one or both shattering to smithereens.

"The Mesopotamians," thought I, "are a savage and lazy race." Approaching what looked like a town or very large cemetery I noticed a person detach himself from the group of human pottery and run to me. Actually it was more of a shuffle than a run, as the light wrapping which swathed him from head to foot incumbered his movements. As he shuffled one of his feet fell off like a dry leaf from a tree.

As he drew near he started shouting: "What news Stranger? What news?"

His appearance was ancient but he was young; the cracked brown face was that of a boy not much older than twelve.

"You are from Bagdad, no doubt?" he asked, panting clouds of dust into my face. I waited to see what I would reply.

"From Bagdad, Master. I have been walking for twenty days."

"Are you dead?"

"No, I think not. The Lord Mayor of Bagdad paid me three farthings to take this present to the Jewish King who lives on the frontier of Hungary. I pass through here as a short cut."

"You are a slave?"

"Why, no," I replied stiffly, "I am a beggar."

"What will you do if you can never get out of the country of the dead? The stone door of Kescke is jealously guarded."

"I will shriek till *doomsday*, till my voice is written all over the center of the earth like the drawings on the wall of a lavatory."

"Still, Kescke may never open."

"Kescke will open."

He put out his tongue, a mere black thread, and uttered a laugh like the last crow of a decrepit rooster.

"What does the Lord Mayor of Bagdad send to the King of the Jews?"

"A toy, Master."

"Besides the toy, what is there in your bag?"

I gave him a cunning smile and shook my matted hair.

"That is a secret, there are twelve thousand treasures in my sack."

Giving another laugh as dry as the wrinkled skin on his

young face he put his head close to my ear and said: "Tell me a story and I will give you a slice of funeral cake."

"Must the story be true?" I asked, setting down my burden.

"All stories are true," he said. "Begin."

———

"One night while passing through the desert by the light of a fat moon I saw a hump on the horizon.

"'That is not a hill,' said I to myself, 'nor yet a town of termites, and I know that the houses of the dead are never fitted into such a form, what can it be?'

"Only my two bare feet could provide the answer so I ate up the caravan track at a great speed, wondering all the while at the changing form of the hump. Before I was near I could make out more humps. They grew in size and complexity till I could see that it was really the encampment of a large caravan.

"Thinking a negligent cook might have left me dinner in an abandoned pot I let myself onto the ground and approached creeping and crawling like an insect.

"The tents, embroidered with foreign letters, were grouped about a central pavilion like chicks around a hen. The pavilion was made of cloth-of-gold inlaid with turquoise spiders.

"A hundred slaves armed with musical instruments squatted all around the tent, blocking my approach. Now and then they twanged, blew or plucked a note, making music which brought my heavy hair upright on my skull.

"A slave passed near the boulder, and with a quick snatch I imprisoned her ankle in my hand. She squeaked like a hen.

"'I am the devil,' I said, 'and you must do my will.'

"'Command,' replied the terrified slave. I could see by her profile and jewels that she was Egyptian.

"'I wish to see your master.'

"'That is difficult,' replied the slave. 'No living being may look at my master for he is the wise King of all the Jews.'

"'If you cannot arrange what I ask I shall release the fire in my fingers and roast you here and now.'

"'Then you must climb onto the royal tent and peep through the hole gnawed by the Chancellor's pet rat.'

"'How shall I pass through the servants and climb such a height without being noticed?'

"'You must disguise yourself as a bird. The King always travels with a drove of Mexican wild turkeys.'

"'Then bring me some feathers.'

"When she had gone I lay in the warm earth which still smelt of the sun. The chill dawn had not yet arrived. Soon the slave returned with a sack of feathers and a jar of honey and I set about disguising myself as a turkey.

"Once I rolled in the honey and the feathers were stuck on, the slave tied a string around my neck and led me through the groups of servants, while I hopped and clucked like an outraged fowl.

"'What have you there?' they asked. 'That is a very ugly bird.'

"'It's a turkey,' replied the Egyptian slave, 'a turkey for the King's supper.'

"Behind the tent hung a silk ladder. The slave indicated this, saying: 'I can help you no more, you must escape as you can when you have seen the King. This was your wish, although you may be cursed to the end of your days for this adventure.'

"'I shall perch on the King's tent and crow my triumph,' I replied. 'The wise King may not pass through the desert till I have seen him.'

"'That is a great impertinence,' said the slave sadly. 'Moses was blasted to bits for less.'

"'Leave me in peace,' I told her. Still shaking her jeweled head, the slave shuffled off to join the other domestics.

"I climbed the silk ladder with some tremor. What if I should be discovered? I startled some vultures which had been sitting immobile on top of the tent, like gourds staring vacantly into the night. They flapped away to a nearby tent to sit once again.

"The Chancellor's pet rat had gnawed a passably large hole in the roof, and without losing a second I peeped through.

"There stood the King admiring himself in a sheet of brass. I could well understand the rapt admiration of the King for his own image. Such a beautiful being never stepped out of a female belly. His great curling beard swept the earth at his feet, black as night herself. The Monarch of all Ravens never had such a majestically curved nose, nor any stag a darker or more liquid eye.

"The nightshirt which hung in long folds from his tall body was embroidered with all the secrets of the cabal in scarlet letters.

"Looking deeply into the face reflected in the sheet of brass the King murmured: 'I am as bored as I am exquisite. Is it a source of pleasure to possess a beauty which cracks any ordinary mirror? Perhaps I eat too much during dinner, perhaps I am depressed because the talking bronze head from Persia will not talk.... I have no new toys and no desire to learn more of the Universe. Play and study are devoid of interest. I am bored and sad ... even fear would be a release.'

"Listening to the King I leaned too far through the hole and fell, landing a few paces from his feet.

"The Monarch leaped into the air with the grace of a goat. The ends of his moustache twitched with fright.

"'An angel of God or Satan?' said the King after he recovered his poise.

"'I am an errant angel banished from Heaven with Lucifer. Out of Hell I crept to find the King of Kings they call Solomon.'

"'No ordinary being may look at me,' replied the King. 'So I must believe you have passed through Heaven and Hell.'

"'I have been feeling a certain soreness in my shoulder blades, which makes me think I'm growing a pair of wings. Creatures eat and become fat . . . I eat and grow wings and become wise.'

"'With what you have learned in Heaven, in Hell, upon and under the Earth, you should possess twelve wings.'

"His words shook me. Dreams and nightmares were contained in the King's hermetic smile.

"I was greatly troubled and I asked: 'You and I can swim back and forth in time, but are we condemned to remain alone?'

"'It is a great thing to be errant in time and space,' said the King. 'The frontiers onto the unknown are constructed in layers. One layer opens into a fan of other layers which open new worlds in their turn. It is true that there is an infinite empty space somewhere beyond the Universe. It is equally true that that space is as richly peopled and inhabited as this very Earth. The space is dark, with no beginning and no end. The space is light, it begins, ends and continues like life.'

"The King sat down and I noticed that a brood of small

transparent roots grew from the soles of his feet. 'Yes, I am also errant. My roots can find no soil and this is why they are visible.'

"'You are a prophet,' I said, 'tell me where is the promised land of the Jews?'

"'Far beyond Mesopotamia and Hungary. Those who find the promised land will be few and they must arrive hundreds of years before and after it has been used as a word. The world only recognizes truth after it is dead and gone . . . I should say a million truths, or a particle of reality.'

"He curled strands of beard in his fingers as he spoke. I was astounded at the shining texture of his whiskers. He continued: 'Words are more useless than the dust of the desert because language has also died, and dead things have movements that are difficult for an eye to perceive.'

"He then gave me a small wooden wheel in the center of which was a spider. 'The eight legs of the spider are love and death. The eight spokes of the wheel are triumph, movement and life.'

"I was shaken by my encounter, and I moved out of the camp without taking any note of my direction. I was sure that I had a mission but I could not remember what it was. As I racked my brain my feet covered great distances; then I realized with a shock that the bearded King was my mission and that I had left him. It was he I had been seeking in Heaven, on Earth and in Hell.

"Shouting insults at myself for my stupidity I turned tail and ran till I felt sick back to where the King had pitched his camp.

"All that remained of the sumptuous camp was a little hole in the dust containing a stick of cinnamon, a skein of black wool and five iron nails."

When I had ended my story, the creature in tight wrappings laughed till he shook and his body rattled like a dry gourd.

"My heart," he explained mirthfully, "is dry as a nut, and rolls about inside me when I laugh."

He gave me a slice of funeral cake as he had promised, and when his mirth had abated I asked: "Is there such a black-bearded King in the great cemetery yonder?"

But the only reply was the frantic rattling of his heart.

The dream left a sensation of such bitter loss that I felt life could only be lived in sleep. Occupations like washing, dressing, eating and talking became so laborious that the sun revolved more slowly on its orbit. Every human creature I saw filled me with repugnance, till I did not dare approach the window to look into the street. When anyone chanced to knock on the door I hid, shuddering with horror in the bathroom. I have never loved my fellow beings but that day the very sight of them became tedious. As long as the light lasted my nerves chattered like parakeets; little by little darkness came and the suffering was less acute. When I saw the lamps' light in the street I went to bed and shortly found myself back in Mesopotamia.

Standing on a hill and looking back along the road I saw the city of tombs still visible in the distance. Before me the road continued like a dusty ribbon whose borders were marked by heaps of broken sculpture and miscellaneous rubbish such as partially unwrapped mummies in different stages of mutilation, painted tablets in every known and unknown language, books and parchments dried into convulsive gestures, old shoes, sandals and boots and any number of pots and casks, urns and dishes in whole or small pieces.

As I walked slowly along the road I examined these rich heaps of rubbish, stopping now and again to root about, putting anything that happened to please me in my sack.

The only tracks in the road leading away from the city were my own. A constant stream of beings passed by all bent on the same destination. Their appearance was confused and some were transparent. There were animals, vegetables, men and women. Some of them had an individual outline but others were joined like siamese twins in two's or three's or in greater numbers, forming geometrical shapes and objects such as five-, six-, eight-, nine- or twelve-sided polygons, triangles, squares, circles, or kitchen utensils and articles of furniture. I saw a five-legged table composed of two terriers, a field of daffodils and three middle-aged women in an embrace. Flapping over them was the carcass of a sea lion.

The motley throng streamed by without noticing me. I supposed they must be ghosts.

After walking some distance putting this and that in my sack I became hungry, and sat down on a Druid's head to eat the funeral cake I had been given in payment for my story. It was hard and dry and difficult to eat. I would have thanked my destiny for a cup of cold water instead, but no liquid was in sight, so I ate what I could and put the rest in my sack for hard times.

Looking back along the road I saw that a vague shape was forming in the distance and advancing in my direction. This gave me some hope for a companion along the lonely road. The thing or person was difficult to define; as it approached it became larger, but it remained a vague form. Only when this fluid and embryonic shape was within a few yards of me could I distinguish a perfect oval containing a moving object within. A light from the center of the object threw out five rays, forming a star. The oval hopped along like somebody walking on one foot, though it did not lack grace.

"That," I said aloud, "is the Egg. The Egg within the Star, the Star within the Egg."

These words seemed appropriate, for it hesitated a few yards away and hopped nimbly onto a painted tombstone, where it perched.

"Our meeting must explain why I lost the black-bearded King. That I know."

This produced no effect on the Egg so I realized that I must dive deeper to find the right words. When I could utter these words the reply would follow as fatally as day follows night.

Taking a small trowel out of my sack I began to dig in the roadside for the word that would open the secret of the Egg. As I worked I repeated all the long words I knew such as federation, conspicuous, anthropology and metamorphosis. The Egg did not budge an inch. I tried one syllable words like am, art, it and off. The Egg trembled very slightly, without communicating any meaning to me. I then understood that the word to address such a primitive and embryonic body would have to come from a language buried at the back of time. The very moment that I understood this my trowel grated on a hard thing in the earth, and with a cry of joy I pulled a small pipe out of the ground. I put it to my lips and blew some notes which started low but mounted the scale rapidly till it reached such a high pitch that my ear could scarcely catch the thin sound. An umbilical cord unrolled slowly out of the center of the Egg and wriggled along the ground towards me. When it reached my left foot I picked up the end and knotted it firmly around my neck. Thus united, the Egg and I started along the road in Indian file. As we advanced I played the pipe. Our movements coincided in a kind of elementary dance, facilitating the journey so much that we travelled far before I felt any fatigue.

A lonely pair we made, the Egg and I, in the great dusty plain of Mesopotamia.

So long as I made my thin tune on the pipe the Egg hopped along behind me willingly, but if I hesitated for a moment it would halt and the umbilical cord would tighten around my neck.

We continued for a long time, until I noticed that the music became slower and the notes lengthened, sounding finally more like shrieks than music. The Egg was drastically affected: the Star stretched and broke the oval contour; each one of the five prongs became a sense and each sense shot out five bright rays which bit into the earth and up into the air like long sharp teeth. The umbilical cord withered and dried till it hung about my neck like a piece of straw.

The Star and the Egg had become a small white child who stood frail and luminous in the road. All that remained of the Star was a five-pronged crown of root and bone on the child's head.

The music had not been still for long when the child spoke: "Be fed by my death; I am half born but my death will be complete. All the colors on Earth have made me white; all the animals under the sky have made my body, but my soul is the rope which hangs from the half circle of light into the half circle of darkness above and below the horizon." When it had spoken the White Child wrapped its hair around its face and walked on ahead of me. I followed in silence, knowing that our steps would go towards the person that I must find.

The country changed gradually into hills and ravines. Occasionally a wan tree became visible here and there. The painted tombstones thinned out to single dots and were replaced by rocks carved into animals or people or sometimes left in their jagged shapes.

The Child and I were alone. The ghosts had disappeared. As we advanced I began to notice high mountains on the horizon, their peaks white with snow. Then far along the road the dust rose and I could distinguish six horsemen riding hell-for-leather in our direction.

The six men were dressed in colored rags and metal jewels, their shaggy horses covered with embroidered blankets haphazardly affixed with chains or rope. As they came they hurled armfuls of Bohemian glass on the road, making a great clatter. The noise of broken glass and the thud of the horses' feet delighted them, and as they ground to a halt in front of the White Child each man shrieked with mirth in six different keys. The foremost of the six men held aloft a wheel. I counted the spokes. They were eight, like a spider's eight legs.

"I am Calabas Kö," said the man who held the wheel. "We have come out of Hungary to take the White Child."

"Then we must move in time," it piped. "I am afraid."

Whereupon one of the men grabbed the Child and tied it to his horse's girth by its hair and they whirled around to gallop back towards the snow-topped mountains.

The morning has been tedious. I have not been able to move away from the window, watching the street, waiting for some sign outside my dreams.

The street is empty and foreign except at night. Outside everything is tainted.

How shall I ever get to the market to buy lunch?

The sign can only appear when I have ceased to need my will. I lurk around the mystery murmuring maledictions on the feebleness of my words.

Hardly daring to touch what I want to say, yet knowing that if I had enough space around me it would be a piercing shriek. White, long, sharp as the crack of a whip.

This is a love letter to a nightmare.

For centuries they dressed up love for easy digestion in the body of a fat little boy with wings, pale blue bows and anaemic looking flowers. Behind this bland decoration Love snarled its rictus through the ages. With shrieks of adoration it flung itself on human breasts, "to crush you, to suck your life away. I cannot drag my own weight over the crust of the earth so you must carry me on your back so that in time you will be cripped with my weight." These words are in every heart in the mating season.

Is this the result of loving a fellow creature? Somewhere I am frightened of my loneliness and feel incomplete with myself.

> Love, goat, tiger...
> Blind Jug, tell the future?
> A time, a date, when?
> "Midnight," replies the Blind Jug.
> Under what sign, Blind Jug?
> "Under the sign of Fire and of Air, Ivory and Milk."
> How many will be to see the Sign?
> "Four, the Moon."
> And how shall we know?
> "Urin, the microscopic ocean."

In some mysterious way these words will enter life.

The air was rare and chill so I thought that I was already amongst the highest mountains. Heavy snow burdened the branches of the fir trees. Streaming grey clouds crept along the earth and about the rocks, leaving icy teeth where they passed.

Built into the mountainside a few yards from me was a great stone door on which was crucified an immense black parrot. As I approached I could see that the bird was still alive, though a long iron nail pierced its heart and the blood oozed out in a scarlet rope. The heavy head hung motionless between its shoulders and the hard yellow eye gave an occasional blink.

"This is the frontier of Hungary," said my thought. "I must walk, swim, creep or sail through the Mountain Kescke to the source of the Danube which flows into Hungary from a subterranean ocean."

The parrot screamed. It began to speak in a rapid nasal voice, but I could see in its eye that it did not understand what it said.

"Anybody who knows may enter but time begins so harness your memory."

It repeated this phrase six times and died.

Try as I would I could find no way to open the door. I kicked and knocked and shouted: "Let me in, Let me in."

The pipe which had enchanted the Egg into motion had disappeared. I was bitterly alone in the land of the dead, on the wrong side of the great stone door.

Several days have passed. I have only slept a few hours, an empty black sleep.

Since the death of the black parrot I have remained alone outside the stone door in the mountain, kicking and knocking and shouting: "Let me in, Let me in."

All through the night I try to get back; to no avail, I can find no means of opening the stone door.

In the daytime I wander about the marketplace thinking, but the Indians keep their world tight and closed over a secret they have probably forgotten for centuries.

The long tentacles of vision and understanding have withdrawn and all that is left is the ragged black hole of my loss. Loss and the world around. A noisy puzzle whose solution is another puzzle noisier and more stupid. The circle widens towards nothing.

An answer is hiding somewhere, if I could only read.

A green shawl has fallen on the arm of a chair. It draws the contours of a horse, a green silk horse, a horse hiding under my shawl.

Lovers get drunk on bitter milk; I am hermaphrodite in love with one of my own dreams. Beast fed with the shade of a dry funeral cake.

Oh Satan, let me love myself again, loving the nightmare of a dead King has made me hate life.

Goodnight, goodnight, I am lost forever in the country of the dead.

Amagoya crept to the black tin trunk and hid the papers. She looked over her shoulder anxiously to make sure that she was alone. Only the striped tom cat watched her activity out of transparent eyes.

Then she took a pen and paper and started to write a letter:

"You left everything here and I read what you had hidden in the trunk. All that is written there partially belongs to me, I cannot apologize for having read your secrets. You always told me everything. . . .

"Do you remember all the strange worlds we crossed together? You should have told me because I possess some of the missing pieces in your story. You say things so much more easily than I, you know that I could never talk well.

"It is impossible to believe that we are now separate persons.

"When I was a child I had bright red hair and I tried to wish it gold. It became dark brown. At night when I was quite sure that everybody had retired I used to light the candle and stand naked before the mirror, wishing myself blond.

"One night while I was watching my naked body in the looking glass and thinking that I resembled an ivory mannikin on a black cloth, which was the dark room behind me, I felt breath on my back and my image was snuffed off the mirror while the lighted candle still flickered in my hand. The darkness formed a new full light of its own and I saw that my reflection was that of a large black dog whose pelt clung dripping wet to his thin body. Before I realized that I had become a dog, I thought that I had turned black by trying to force myself blond.

"Perhaps you will know the meaning of all this, for I confess that I am puzzled yet, I feel that I must tell you...."

Amagoya shook the powdery snow out of her fur and looked about for her bedroom. The walls had dissolved into mountainous countryside and the ceiling had arched into the sky.

She was standing on the fringe of a forest and she found that her eyes could penetrate far through the mass of trees to a house which winked its lights like candles. A will from inside the house pulled her into the forest and she let it guide her along a narrow path, trodden by hoof and paw.

The drive gates hung wearily off their hinges, so she walked through soundlessly and looked up at the house which squatted against the sky like a carved box. A lighted tower was sharply drawn against the sky; upon its summit pranced a centaur whose arrow pointed towards the east.

Amagoya sat down in the snow and howled at the moon because three wills were pulling at her spirit and the pain was worse than giving birth to a litter of pups. She felt the wills like burning wire; they pulled her apart in three directions.

Then two of these wills withdrew and she was sucked into the house by the third and up a spiral staircase like a reversed whirlpool to the white skirt of an old Chinaman. A few moments after she had entered, the light faded and they were covered with darkness. She heard herself pattering down the spiral staircase, drawn after the Chinaman.

Below they entered a round chamber which was lit by an oval globe suspended from the ceiling. The light was hard and bright like that of an operating theatre.

Amagoya could see that there were two other persons beside the Chinaman. Their outlines were blurred to her eyes, but she could distinguish that one was fat and the other thin. The Chinaman however, was visible in three dimensions and seemed to attract the light to his body.

"Why have we come in here?" asked the thin one. Amagoya could smell the fear that rose off his body like steam.

The Chinaman and the fat man sat down while the other remained standing. The door, thick and padded like the door of a safe, had closed silently behind them.

"You are to return from whence you came," said the Chinaman. "Your desires do not correspond with the plan upon which this earth is conceived."

"The plan is stale and has been so now for many centuries. Only the mixture of male and female can make a living being."

"The plan will not change. If the omnipotent power fell into multiple hands, the working system would automatically disintegrate."

"The earth must be renewed. . . ."

"You have spoken enough," said the Chinaman. He pulled his stool to the center of the room and turned his eyes inward. The fat person pulled twelve wires out of the round wall and gave them to the Chinaman, who took them like the reins of a team of horses.

As soon as the Chinaman held the wires, Amagoya heard the thumping of a great heart and the rumbling of the digestive organs of some huge body. This was followed by the sound of many distant voices quarreling in tongues. Then she could hear the cries of wild beasts and birds, the whistling of wind, the rushing of water, the sizzling of fire and the angry grumbling of the minerals of the earth at boiling point, heaving under their crust of mountains like an enormous child struggling for birth.

All of a sudden the Chinaman twisted the wires and knotted them together. Silence fell. Amagoya could feel her veins clog with stopped blood. "So you see," said the Chinaman releasing the wires, "all is usual."

The noise decreased and faded away to a murmur and then nothing. Amagoya could see the tall blurred figure standing straight and rigid in front of the Chinaman; she could feel the bitter smell of his fear and the tension of the resistance he opposed to the other's will. Her spirit twisted and entered the struggle and she was pulled between the two wills like a piece of silk thread. Staring at the back of the Chinaman's shaven head, she tried to wrench herself back into her own body.

"I may undergo a change so complete that my very bones might become another substance," said the thin person. He disappeared slowly as he spoke.

"You will remain immobile for all eternity."

"Eternity is a long time. I shall be born again."

"If you are born again, I shall take measures to blast you off the face of the Earth."

"You will never find me."

The Chinaman made a long slit of a smile and replied: "Jew, you will come to me of your own accord and choice."

"If what you say is true, then I will come to tear the power out of your hands and throw it to the four winds so that the Earth and the plan of the Earth can be renewed."

In the darkness and screams that followed, Amagoya pressed her belly to the floor to ease the pains that seared her bowels.

Like one blind eye the moon appeared at the open window to light and empty the room. All that remained of the scene she had witnessed was a very small golden cage which contained an ivory doll.

Taking the cage between her teeth, Amagoya leapt out of the window onto the snow outside and ran away from the house. Finding herself once more in the forest she ran about aimlessly. She ran around so long and without thinking that her feet were sore and weary when she decided to dig herself into the snow and sleep.

She dreamed that she was human once more and had grown into a woman. Dressed in rich clothes of puce and purple velvet she was riding through the forest on a bicycle. A person, either a young man or woman, ran at her side laughing at her.

Amagoya looked at her discreetly and decided that she was a hermaphrodite. Against her breast, the hermaphrodite carried the golden cage which contained the ivory doll.

"Who are you and where are we going?" asked Amagoya pedalling for all she was worth. "And why am I dreaming you?"

"Who am I and where are we going! What a lot of questions all at once. I hardly know which to answer first! To answer who I am would be difficult because I scarcely know; sometimes it is quite precise though every time I am a different person. Perhaps you are dreaming me because I am part of yourself or part of your life, although how do you know that it is not I who am dreaming you?

"To answer the third question you asked about our destination . . . we are going to see a simple Artisan because the bird in this cage is no ordinary bird and I wish to know his virtues."

"Have you got the bird? It is not a bird but an ivory doll."

By this time they had reached a high yew hedge which enclosed a large and beautifully cultivated garden. It was neither day nor night but something which resembled twilight or early dawn. They stood together on a lawn looking towards a house.

"This is the house of the Artisan," she explained. "She is a doll maker, an artist."

Out of the house ran a nimble figure about the same height as a five-year-old child. Amagoya saw at once that the Artisan was a dwarf and a hunchback.

"Did you find it Brigit?" she asked breathlessly. "Ah, I see you did . . . where?"

"Under the dead body of a black dog," replied Brigit. "In a hole in the snow. They were almost buried."

"And who is this?" asked the Artisan examining Amagoya with some curiosity. "Did you also find her in the snow?"

"Yes," replied Brigit, "she was sitting on the ground crying near the body of the dog."

The Artisan chuckled to herself as if she had a secret joke. "It is prejudice that makes us conceive time as a straight line," she told Amagoya, "or as any sort of line at all, from a corkscrew to a zig-zag, or a circle or anything really. Time was invented as something strictly beginning and ending irrevocably, a long time after they made clocks. It is erroneous to think that two necessarily follows one and that twice three is eternally condemned to make six. I forgot how to count long ago because as soon as I reasoned a while I saw I had to start everything all over again, and real counting did not fit at all into the strict stiff rules mathematicians made for us. Never mind, we shall see a delightful chaos soon! Here I am talking my head off when we have so much to do, come along my children."

She took Amagoya by the hand and hurried towards the house. "I have been too busy to look after the garden; it is a pity you shall not see it at its best. Never mind though, it is a peaceful spot and perhaps you will again?"

They entered a large hall full of dolls, mannikins in every sort of wood, bone, ivory, clay or porcelain; figures of animals, plants and birds carved in the most delicate styles. There were clay dolls from every country in the world, some in the form of foetuses. Others had the body of a praying mantis or the face of a Borgia.

There were tables, chairs and clocks from two centimeters to eight yards high. Models of houses and gardens, astronomical and mathematical instruments all in varied dimensions.

The Artisan pulled an enormous bouquet of keys out of her bosom and opened a turquoise box which contained an ivory mannikin identical in size and shape to the one in the golden cage.

Amagoya would have liked to stroll around the great hall for a week looking at each object in turn. She thought that it would be like seeing the world through a mirror.

She had hardly time, however, to glance around her when the Artisan pulled her hand impatiently and said "Hurry, there is no time to lose, we must go to the laboratory." She had wrapped both dolls carefully together in a square of pure linen.

The laboratory was reached by descending a flight of stairs which led under the foundations of the house. They entered a vaulted chamber which looked more like a kitchen than a laboratory. The shelves which reached from floor to ceiling were laden with all manner of curious instruments, untidily mixed with over-turned tins of flour or raisins, strings of sausages, dry herbs and half-gnawed hams. Some test tubes and beacons contained used tea leaves, while a highly perfected theodolite might be decorated like some eccentric Christmas tree with vegetables and pieces of string. A fire blazed behind the largest hearth Amagoya had ever seen. Cats of every kind and shape sat in groups gazing into the flames; or they perched on the shelves washing their faces or stalking delicately through bottles, instruments, tins and food. Under and on the tables and chairs were cats; cats in every corner watching everything.

The Artisan cleared a table of numerous cats and bustled about putting things in their places to which, for some reason, they appeared to belong. As she worked she muttered to herself: "We shall soon know who they are; now let me see, in what language would one talk to Ivory? Ah yes, I think I know... Really one can talk to and be answered by everything if one finds the right sound. After all the primary quality of a word is its sound." She placed a white cloth on the table and spread it out smoothly, then she unwrapped the dolls and placed them side by side in the exact center of the cloth.

"Brigit," she said, "fetch me the singing instrument off the shelf."

This was an object entirely constructed of glass tubes and globes, all connected intricately in a system of branches. The whole instrument stood about a yard and a half high. The Artisan walked around examining it closely from all angles and finally rubbed her hands together as if satisfied.

"Now Brigit," she said, "run to the dairy and bring me three gallons of new milk."

Amagoya watched these preparations with interest; she had no doubt that their meaning would become clear before the Artisan had finished.

"I am an old woman," the Artisan told her, "and though I have neither chick nor child I have mothered many thousands of lost souls. I can hear many things and my eyes are sharp. Even the life beating inside a stone is audible to me and that is a gift. I have trained all the love in my body into energy, and all my hate, which is also a great force, I have trained into thought. My womb is no larger than a grain of rice because its powers have all been used in discovery. I say discovery because creation is the finding of something which always existed, existed in a different form or forms but was nevertheless already there, whole or in small pieces waiting to come into being."

"Have you never missed the ordinary functions of a female, loving a man or bearing children?"

"That is a difficult question to which I could answer yes or no. If I passed through the pleasure and suffering of a female animal I would become a different creature. Pleasures and pains can be lived in the past or future. The knowledge of them is already here."

Brigit returned with a great pot in her hand containing three gallons of new milk. Amagoya thought that she must be very strong because her step was light, as if she carried nothing at all.

"It is a question of balance," replied the Artisan to her thoughts. "Weight and lightness are resolved by balance; if you knew how, you could make a hippopotamus perch on your little finger. It is a question of distribution of vital energy."

Brigit had started to pour the milk into the instrument by means of a funnel; it ran through the tubes like blood through the veins of a live body. When she had emptied the pot, the milk continued to move through the tubes of its own accord. The instrument was so constructed that it kept any liquid poured inside it in perpetual motion. While Brigit poured the milk the Artisan attached a long transparent and flexible tube around the two dolls and inserted the other extremity into a branch of the glass instrument. They waited in silence while the milk trickled on its way through the glass twigs, globes and branches.

The two ivory dolls twitched slightly on the table. Although the silence was complete, they could hear a rhythmic sound made by the milk on its perpetual and mysterious journey. The twitching of the dolls increased until one of them finally succeeded in taking an upright position; the other, as if encouraged by its success, followed its example and they stood together, swaying in the center of the white cloth.

"That will do for the milk," said the Artisan, "it is only part of the alchemy of Ivory."

Brigit pulled a rubber stopper out of the instrument and all the milk flowed into a large bowl on the floor. A legion of cats agglomerated at once and cleaned up the milk.

The Artisan held the transparent tube pinched between her fingers while the two dolls tottered uncertainly at the other end.

"Hurry Brigit," she said, "they are in movement. Bring the Mercury."

Soon the instrument was filled with flowing quicksilver and not only could they hear the silent song it made, but they also heard the invisible life of the dolls and their voices. They could feel and touch the sensations of the mannikins, although to the sharpest ear not a sound could be heard.

Amagoya could now understand the voice of the Artisan as she spoke to the ivory dolls through the quicksilver.

"Mercury speaks to Ivory; hear me, I am the Artisan but I am also Mercury. My voice is human and mineral, your two Ivory bodies are one whole body. Ivory the weapon, Saturn the body, hear me and speak."

Then addressing the first doll: "Where are you?"

First Doll: I am a prisoner in my Ivory body which was once flesh and bone.

Artisan: Who are you, Ivory Doll?

First Doll: I am a Jew and I no longer believe what I have said, done or thought.

Artisan: Do you know your destiny?

First Doll: I must be born again to find my sister Fire, who is also a Ram, a woman and a gentile.

The Artisan then addressed herself to the second doll who quivered like a needle on a compass.

Artisan: Where are you, Ivory Doll?

Second Doll: Let me in, Let me in, I shall die of cold.

Artisan: Since you are alive, why are you amongst the dead?

Second Doll: I am seeking my brother Air who passed through Mesopotamia in the form of a Hebrew King.

Artisan: Your brother must deliver you from the dead. I cannot create or control destiny, my power merely serves to free destinies so that they can fly over their own route. Although I can enter and become any matter, there is no matter I can control or dominate because I am without a will. The power within me is free of my person.

Second Doll: Let me in, Let me in, I am suffering bitterly.

The Artisan released the Mercury which flowed onto the floor and into every nook, hole and corner, a heavy silver stream.

The dolls fell flat on their faces and she picked them up tenderly, wrapped them in a red cloth and flung them both into the center of the fire. A great gust of wind whistled through the chamber sending the flames leaping up the chimney. When the wind died away the flames sunk back into the cinders out of which escaped a glittering green beetle and a speckled partridge which flew up the chimney.

"So" said the Artisan, "all is ended; that is to say that all has commenced and shall be forever renewed. They will meet again in and out of time, having changed bodies."

She lit a small clay pipe and walked away up the stairs, smoking pensively and humming to herself as she went.

3

PHILLIP and Michelle were in the kitchen making their dinner. A lamb stew bubbled on the fire and they both added ingredients according to their fantasy. The reddish grease on the surface of the stew heaved like lava in the crater of a live volcano.

"I am going to add a few dried plums and raisins," said Phillip stirring the mixture, "and some more cream which will make the taste suave. It is a trifle too sharp." Michelle nodded absently and went on hunting for the pepper.

"What do you say if I chopped some garlic and raw ham? The mutton here is very strong and dominates the whole taste like a bassoon in a whole orchestra of harps."

"I say that you always do what you please whatever opinion I offer, so why ask?" she replied. She had found the pepper and was shaking it vigorously into the thick, bubbling stew.

"That isn't true," said Phillip, "because if I always did what I pleased we would have parted long ago."

He was thinking that there was no real reason why he should not add a few handfuls of red cabbage to the general harmony, for cooking was as infinite a complication as the most incomprehensible form of higher mathematics. The same precision and nicety were essential to a perfectly constructed dish. A humble pound of mutton prepared by knowing fingers could evoke the green hills of paradise to an educated palate. Taste, he thought, has a system of ecstasy and philosophy all its own which is in no way inferior to the gifts of the other four senses. Pleased with his thoughts he replied absently: "Oh, that's quite another matter."

"Why is it another matter?" He was already chopping the red cabbage into lacy pink-purple strips. They knew each other so well now that it was becoming obscene. What demon made them walk so easily in and out of each other's private minds, stealing thoughts before they were even formulated? He found it irritating.

"Why is it another matter?"

"Because you need me and you know quite well nothing ever succeeds for you when I am not there."

"That is a painful truth and I am too intelligent not to know that I shall never be master of my destiny. That applies to everyone. Where are the tomatoes?"

She scraped the bottom of the pot through the unctuous gravy, which already showed a tendency to burn.

"Why do they call tomatoes 'pommes d'amour'?"

"Probably because they resemble certain unmentionable portions of the masculine anatomy."

"Here you are," she said. "Fat and ripe; they are just the same red as Chinese lacquer."

Phillip started and dropped a wooden spoon on the floor, spattering the hem of his trousers with mutton fat.

"What ever are you doing? Now I shall have to send them to the cleaners."

There were some things she did not know.

"What time did you tell them to come? Did Guadalupe fetch the wine?"

"You will miss someone this evening," said Michelle, watching him over her shoulder. "It will seem strange to see them without her. Somehow I think that she isn't done with us yet, though to all appearances she has disappeared from our lives. Even if we meet, she will seem far away. Still I continue to be convinced she has not done with us."

"What do you mean?" The heat of the kitchen made him sweat, and his odor filled the little room.

"You know what I mean; whenever you reply with a question I know it's because you want to gain time to think out an evasive reply."

"Perhaps you are right, but it is bad policy to show all one's knowledge at once."

"I tried to find out from Amagoya but she is very discreet."

"You seem to be more absorbed in the question than its importance seems to merit."

"I don't think you are speaking the truth."

"My dear, you are morbidly preoccupied with the truth."

The stew simmered on a very low fire and gave up complicated, succulent aromas: herbs, vegetables and fruits delicately mixed with the slight wild beast smell of Mexican mutton.

She went out for a few seconds to lay the table. They had a large modern room decorated with a few savage objects spaced at prim intervals on the wall. This neat arrangement gave the uncouth objects the aspect of ordinary ornaments.

The fat woman laid the table for four people and returned to the kitchen thinking of the fifth place that would not be occupied.

"Last night I dreamt that she returned. You got out and followed her into the street in your pajamas. Taking care not to be seen, I followed you both a short distance. You walked in the Bosque of Chapultepec arm-in-arm. Your voices were low but they came to me quite clearly.

"You did a very strange thing. You took a Jew's harp out of your pocket and played quite ravishingly, and she danced around, clapping her hands and crying: 'Ah yes! isn't it beautiful!'

"When you had finished you suddenly grabbed her by the hair and swung her around over your head shouting: 'Traitress! Strumpet! How nearly you made me believe!'

"Her screams were high and shrill like a bird, and when you released her she flew out of your arms in the form of a small speckled partridge. You laughed and turned back in my direction saying: 'I knew you were there all the time.'"

"A peculiar dream," said fat Phillip. "Do you think we ought to boil some potatoes?"

"Yes I really think so, otherwise there's too much sauce. For some reason people seem embarrassed to mop up their plates with bread."

"Do you know what a dragon signifies?" he asked after tasting the sauce. "Because last night I dreamt about a dragon."

"It may have different meanings," replied the woman. "What sort of a dragon did you dream?"

Phillip sniffed the sauce critically and sprinkled in a pinch of salt before replying.

"I expect it was a Chinese dragon. You know most dragons seem to be Chinese. It was a very small one, no larger than a tabby cat and quite black. I cooked it in a cream sauce and the taste was rather like that of a squid. That would probably be correct if one ever had the opportunity of eating a dragon. A squid is really more of a reptile than a fish."

"Was that all?" asked the woman. "If so, it seems the greedy dream of a little boy."

"Dragons are really reptiles," he continued pensively, "and reptiles are nearer to birds than fish. Birds are somehow sinister with their feathery bodies, sharp beaks and skeleton legs. When I was a child I was terrified of birds. Even today I cannot repress my satisfaction when I eat chicken, almost as if I have disposed of an enemy. Have you ever looked into a parrot's eye? Did you ever notice that it blinks the wrong way? I forget if all birds have the same peculiarity, that image is tied to the parrot."

"When I was a little girl I thought chickens were the souls of dead actresses."

"Yes, now I remember how my dream began; I was standing outside the British Museum waiting for somebody who, I think, was to give me access to some precious documents I had been anxious to see for a great number of years. A thick London fog enveloped the entrance gates and so I could not clearly see the people who came and went from the Museum. As I waited, somewhat impatiently, I passed the time examining the big sculpture from Easter Island which guards the door like a dead sentry. At that moment my back was turned to the street, so I was startled when somebody placed a hand on my shoulder. Turning quickly I faced the stranger whom I had never seen, though it was clear to me he was the man for whom I had been waiting with such impatience. He seemed to be dressed in dark clothes and the peculiarity I noticed at once, without any surprise, was that his face had neither eyes nor mouth; instead the features were only indicated faintly on a pale surface. Although he had no mouth, he could speak in a somewhat muffled voice: 'You must excuse me,' he said, taking his watch out of his pocket and feeling the hour with his fingers, 'I am late but I was detained on business in the City.'

"'Not at all,' I said politely, 'I was very interested studying this person from Easter Island.'

"'Entirely magnificent,' he replied. 'England has many treasures.' This was obviously my opportunity so I offered him a cigar, wondering as I did so where he would smoke it. He refused.

"'Yes, England is a wonderful place because everything is intact. Those documents you spoke of are quite unique for their kind. I always knew that I would find them in England.'

"'Ah quite, but of course that is the reason you came to England? Have you seen the Tower of London? There are some wonderful sights here for tourists.'

"I told him that I had not seen the Tower of London. During this conversation I found that we were already inside the Museum and were hurrying past the Elgin Marbles. Finally he led me into a gallery which had shelves on either side packed with documents.

"'All these are at your disposal,' he told me. 'You are at liberty to make your own choice, but I could be of more assistance if you would tell me exactly what you wish to see.'

"He had taken off his hat and I saw that his faint white forehead was decorated with a brilliant decagonal jewel.

"'You know what I wish to see.'

"'He coughed discreetly from some invisible orifice in his body. 'Of course I must surmise that you are in England because you are no longer content with the ancient order of things? Naturally we were already informed that the triangle was no longer intact and subsequently we waited for you day after day, having surmised that your first movement would be in the direction of Great Britain. The disorder following your mistake has been most inconvenient for us here in England, but we are nonetheless prepared to study any logical change you are disposed to propose. Of course it would be useless to accentuate the fact that the change in question must not affect the present powers too radically or create any visible outward manifestation. The formula of preparation for almost every Coming in most of the countries of this planet is enumerated in detail amongst the documents you see here.'

"'Of course they all deal with the past?' I asked, waiting for his reply with some apprehension. 'The distant past?'

"'Naturally,' he replied. 'They deal with a past further away than the beginning of writing.'

"I felt uncomfortable, as though he were watching me closely out of his eyeless face.

"'Perhaps it would be equally true,' I continued nervously, 'to say that the documents that treat of the darkest past could cast some light on the immediate future?'

"'The word is prophetic.'

"It was like the game 'Animal, Vegetable and Mineral.' He had already moved to one of the shelves and was taking out a folio of ancient aspect. The cover seemed to be primitively bound with dry leaves and scraps of untanned skin.

"Placing the book on the table near the window he said: 'Before you peruse the substance of this document I wish to inform you that the content thereof is His Majesty's property and cannot be used or understood without the consent of the entire British Empire. It is a formula,' he added, 'to which we have to adhere according to the rules imposed by the Board of the Museum.'

"We both screamed as he opened the cover of the folio, for all the pages were gnawed away to ugly scraps of lace, and in the middle of the lacerated document sat a small black dragon. For a moment it seemed stunned by the light, then all of a sudden it flickered free from the ruin it had wrought and started to scuttle off the table. With a rapid movement the man snatched it by the tail and walloped its head vigorously on the stone floor till it appeared to be dead.

"'They do a great deal of damage,' he said, holding the limp black dragon in his hand. 'The Procurator had forty traps delivered last week. They continue nevertheless to molest us and I believe that we shall be obliged to use poison. Well, never mind . . .' he ended. 'They have the virtue of being edible and as I do not wish you to return empty handed from your arduous expedition I would be edified if you would accept this with my personal and exclusive compliments.'

"To my horror he handed me the dragon's carcass and in ordinary courtesy I felt that I was obliged to accept."

"That is all, be careful, I smell burning, the stew will be spoiled."

Phillip scraped the bottom of the pot with a wooden spoon.

4

"ALWAYS be dignified, remember to be polite. You are going to study and learn many things which will help you in the world. Now you must blow your nose, so...."

Rebecca demonstrated the adult method of blowing a nose in a huge white handkerchief, rubbing her streaming eyes impatiently as she did so. They were already red and sore.

"Remember that you are a Jew and always remember this with pride and dignity, no matter what the world outside may do or say."

She was kneeling before her little boy putting on his socks. He was passive and soft with sleep and watched her face with wide black eyes.

"My fingers fumble so with the cold. Stretch your foot, Zacharias."

Grandmother came in and placed a brown paper parcel in the child's hands. He clutched it to his bosom like a doll.

"It's seven o'clock daughter, you must hurry. They will be waiting. Is he ready?"

Rebecca nodded and scrambled heavily to her feet. "I will get my shawl. Aaron, Aaron, are you dressed?"

"Yes Mother." The other boy appeared in the doorway and stared in awe at his brother. Rebecca hurried out.

"Will he ever come back, Grandmother?"

"Yes of course, child. He will return a great learned man."

"Is he going far away from Budapest?"

"Hold your tongue Aaron."

There was silence for a while as she bustled about the room making small packages.

"Grandmother?"

"Are you a child or a parrot? Always talk, talk, talk."

Aaron was startled and relapsed into silence. They hurried along on the slippery pavement. A horse drawing a sledge trotted past, tinkling agitated little bells. Aaron wished that they could be riding behind the horse and its gay bells, but he did not dare speak for he was frightened of the terrible stranger his mother had become. She strode along, dragging the children at her side with her cold hands, her face almost invisible inside the black shawl.

The sun was up as they arrived at a square building whose large doors stood open to a crowd of Jewish women and their children. Some were in rags and some, like Rebecca, were dressed in threadbare but respectable clothes, held together precariously by much diligent mending.

Two long benches in the bare entrance hall accommodated the women, while an attendant hustled the children through a stained glass door.

When he came to Rebecca she clutched her son roughly and kissed him once between the eyes. Then looking up at the attendant she asked: "Shall I wait?" He was a young man with a forlorn moustache and empty blue eyes.

"As you please." He seemed impatient and stood with a hand on the boy's shoulder as if wishing to be gone.

"Name?" He scribbled in a shiny little red book. "Address?" And after a short hesitation he asked: "Are you a widow?"

Rebecca had hardly time to nod before her son was hustled

through the stained glass door and disappeared after the other little boys.

They went down a passage which smelt acridly of poverty and some strong disinfectant. The walls, distempered green, were occasionally decorated with prints of the largest monuments in Budapest in brown and white.

About a hundred and fifty boys were seated on wooden chairs in a long chilly room. Five men with shears and white aprons passed with surprising rapidity from child to child, shaving each small head to a grey stubble. The floor was covered with dark curly hair, as if a flock of black sheep had been shorn to their skins. When the hair cutting had finished they hurried the children to the baths. Each child made a small packet of his home clothes which were afterwards given back to their parent or relations.

Because he was only four, the youngest of all the children, Zacharias was dressed after the bath by the forlorn attendant. He was put into long striped trousers of a harsh material and a jacket buttoned up to the chin with the number 105 sewn on the left sleeve in the same place where people wear the black band of mourning. Each foot was folded in a square of navy blue calico and pushed into a pair of brand new boots made of rigid black leather. When he stood on his feet he looked like some oddly dressed puppet made by a mad doll maker.

Once the shearing, bathing and dressing were over the children streamed back through the stained glass doors. Some clattered to their parent's sides while others stood about self-consciously in their new stiff clothes stamping their shiny boots.

Rebecca took her child in her arms and kissed his face and hands.

"Be a good boy, be a good boy." She could think of nothing else to say. "I'll come and visit you soon. Be a good boy."

Then taking Aaron by the shoulders she pushed him into the street and they hurried away as they had come.

He tried to run after her but his new boots slipped on the stone flags and he fell on his face. He was picked up, crying bitterly. At that time he did not mind that others saw him cry and the tears came easily.

An hour later when they were on the train bound for the Northern mountains he vomited all the breakfast grandmother had given him over his new trousers and shiny black boots.

105 sat up in bed and screamed. A hundred and forty-nine children stirred, murmured or sat up, then sank back to sleep as they understood that it was only another of 105's frequent nightmares.

105, however, did not follow their example. He could not go back to sleep. He lay sweating in his narrow bed, pinching his thighs through the coarse night shirt. He knew it was against regulations to put one's arm under the cover: the offence was severely punished.

The long dormitory did not offer a rich field of contemplation. Beds in two rows against either wall were divided by a strip of linoleum which was worn thin down to the middle. The oblong windows, placed much too high to look out, let in a pale light when there was a moon. Then the linoleum glistened and 105 pretended that it was the Danube and his bed was a boat that would sail him back to Budapest. Tonight however, there was no boat. The Horror was too near, it was inside him, all around and over the bed.

Once at a local fair he had crawled unobserved into the chamber of horrors; he had been attracted by a serious-looking black and white printed card which said: "ADULTS ONLY." The boys had been strictly forbidden to enter. For once in his life 105 regretted having broken one of the rules of the Institution.

Inside was an orgy of horror. A beautiful lady lay in her nightdress on a silk bed. She was made of wax and looked so much alive that 105 turned back several times to see if she had moved. In her long golden hair sat a demon, a dwarf, a monkey, and a serpent. He whispered temptations into her pale pink ear. After this came colored photographs of people eaten away by syphilis, unborn foetuses in different stages, and finally a scene from the Spanish Inquisition which had haunted him ever since: at night he was constantly apprehensive that it should return.

As his memory of this scene became older it gathered in detail and richness, finally far surpassing the original in fantasy and horror. It usually began with a vaulted cellar furnished with a somewhat confused assembly of giant meat-mincers, iron armchairs with adjustable spikes in the seat and back, long man-shaped boxes, and a thing which looked like a monster sewing machine with a needle as long as a man's body and stained with clots of blood. This object awoke the painful memory of his mother's sewing machine; she earned their living as a dressmaker. From early morning to late night during the short holidays she pedalled away on expensive yards of soft material belonging to somebody else. 105 went stiff with hate when he thought of the monotonous chuffing of the sewing machine. His mother seemed to pedal away on a long painful journey, leaving him when he wanted to tell her so many important things and the time was so short. She pedalled away to Poland, where his father lay dead under the snow.

Somewhere in the thick mobile shadows a door clicked so audibly that he jumped. Eight pale-faced priests scampered lightly about the terrible vaulted chamber, pressing buttons and twirling handles; they were trying out the machines. They were going to sew him into a bloody pair of combinations for a little cream-faced Spanish Prince.

105 screamed and the vision disappeared abruptly, leaving him weak with terror and determined not to fall asleep till dawn. Then for hours he fought not to see the picture lurking in the back of his mind. He tried to evoke the Danube at midday, or another more powerful spell against the moonfaced priests.

Walking up a long avenue of trees towards a castle whose windows were glittering orange squares. Walking: but if all went well he would be wafted off his feet at the fifth tree. Counting them as he passed: one, two, three, four, five; then deliciously wafted off his feet a short distance off the ground. It was not really flying because he used no effort at all. It was being lifted by some power not his own.

The doors of the castle opened as he approached and in the vague interior stood a bright pink damsel. Her high coloring resembled a rose colored sweet called "Krumpli Cukor" made out of sugar and potatoes which 105 had eaten on several memorable occasions. The bright pink sweetmeat quality of the lady was mixed with something else no less fascinating and which he dimly recognized as being female. Trembling with a strange warmth which began in his cheeks and which crept heavily downwards, 105 drifted into her arms. The caress was unlike anything that he had ever known; this, he imagined, was woman, the faraway skirted creature who held the unique power over loneliness, nightmares and warmth.

As he lay with tightly closed eyes trying to evoke the pink lady something touched his arm and said: "Shhhh." He kept his eyes closed and waited. Something sat on the bed, it bent and kissed his cheek.

"You had another," whispered the voice. "I know you are not asleep, so don't pretend."

99 sat shivering beside him.

"You'll catch cold," said 105, relieved and disappointed. And if the Lurcher takes a midnight stroll, you'll get a beating."

"Let me get in your bed," said 99. "I'm cold."

"No," said 105. "There isn't room. I can't even turn over myself without nearly falling on the floor."

"All right then I'll stand, even if I do catch pneumonia. Let's talk."

"The Lurcher will catch us. It isn't worthwhile."

"I feel cold inside too and I can't feel my feet anymore."

"Then go back to bed."

"Look, I've got a present for you," said 99, pressing five iron nails into 105's hand. "They're the heavy kind and hardly rusted at all. I traded them with 62 for my green toothbrush. He wanted it to clean machinery."

Iron nails were used for a game called Boki which consisted of throwing nails into the air and catching them with various methods. Horseshoe nails were the most prized—and these were the kind 99 gave to 105. He tied them cautiously into the corner of his nightshirt and thanked 99.

"Now please go to bed, tomorrow I'll let you see my compass."

The little boy crept silently back to his own bed and soon afterwards 105 fell asleep.

He dreamt that he was walking up a drive bordered with tufted green trees. The place was quite different from the residence of the Pink Lady and the flowering shrubs along each side of the avenue were a kind he had never seen. Hearing the sound of hooves beating on the gravel, he hid behind a bush and waited. A little girl rode into view on a fat Shetland pony. She joggled up and down on the saddle chanting: "Gee up Bessie! Gee up!" The pony suddenly broke into a gallop and rushed past 105 at an astonishing pace for such a beast.

"She never galloped before," he heard the little girl say. "She's too fat even to trot properly."

When they had disappeared around a bend in the drive, 105 stepped out of his hiding place and followed the direction taken by the girl and pony.

He met them returning rather slowly. The girl looked surprised, and her mouth hung open.

"Who are you?" she said. "I hadn't counted you in and there you are, uninvited like Tomey."

105 felt embarrassed and his head seemed full of numbers. "She is younger than I," he said to himself.

"Who are you?" asked the girl again. "I knew I was going to dream of Black Bess but I hadn't counted in anyone else. It's rude. I don't know you, do I?"

"Yes, you do!" shouted 105. "You know you do, how could you have forgotten? Remember the five horseshoe nails you gave me?"

She frowned and looked puzzled, then after a while she said: "No, you left them for me and I never could give them back." She began to cry for no reason, and wiped away her tears with her hair.

"Who are you? Who are you? I can't remember you, you must tell me."

"Who are you then?" replied 105, "and why do we go on asking all the time when we know."

"We know but we can't remember," said the little girl. "What else did you give me? There were two other things I know."

105 shook his head. "It's too far away to remember precisely...."

Then she jumped off the pony and hopped around chanting: "If you can't guess you'll have to go away, it's a game."

"The nails were enough for today," said 105. "Is this your garden?"

"It's my father's garden. We use it all the time but he hardly ever does, he works."

"Where are we?" asked 105. "I mean what country?" The little girl rolled about cackling with mirth: "Ha ha ha, he doesn't even know where he is, ha ha ha, what an ignoramus!"

"Stop that or I'll twist your arm till you plead for mercy."

She stopped obediently and put her lips to his ear: "We're in England, of course, SILLY!" suddenly jumping away after shouting the last word into his eardrum.

"England?" said 105, turning the world over in his mind. "Of course, you are in England now, and I am in Hungary."

"Of course," said the girl and stopped suddenly, staring at him. "In Hungary, in Hungary, now I seem to remember something. How old are you?"

105 was going to say that he was twelve but different words came out of his mouth: "Very old."

"I'm six," she said. "But I'm in my seventh year."

The pony had disappeared and they had turned off the drive into a wood.

"We are going to the Big Pond." She ran in front of him, leading the way. "They don't allow us to go when we're awake, but in dreams you do what you want unless they're nightmares. Jim Gardner says the Big Pond has no bottom." They were pushing through rhododendrons to a small lake covered with floating green weed: "Nanny says they're called rodidandrums, Jackie had some in the garden in Ireland and my sister-in-law had blue ones. There aren't any blue rodidandrums in England."

They sat together near the water on the moss.

"This is a dangerous place," said the girl. "It's haunted. That's why Gerard and I love to come here. Gerard is my younger brother."

"So you are not alone." 105 felt cheated.

"Yes I am!" she said violently. "They all hate me because I'm a girl. Little girls can't do the same things as little boys, they say. It isn't true. I can kick harder than Gerard and I don't allow him to draw horses. Mummy told me I have such a bad temper that I'll be an old witch before I'm twenty. I don't care if I do wrinkle up before I'm twenty, I'll still climb trees and come to the Big Pond whenever I like."

The stagnant coat of weed seemed to shift, but the girl took no notice: "I have three brothers, one mother and one father. They all do whatever they like because they are boys. It isn't fair. When I grow up I'll shave and put hair oil on my face to grow a beard. Pat has a moustache and at school he says they call him Bobby whiskers. He says he kicks them whenever they call him that. Once I called him Bobby whiskers and he kicked me. I'm the only one that has to practice the piano for hours, wash all day and say thank you for everything. You should see the clothes they make me wear."

105 started to laugh. He couldn't stop, and the tears rolled down his cheeks till he didn't know if he was laughing or crying. The little girl stared at him horrified, then scrambled to her feet and ran away. 105 was panic-stricken. He leapt to his feet and followed her as fast as he could. When he caught her she was crying and struggling in his arms: "Let me go you Damn Pig!"

"Shut up," said 105. "You're nothing more than a silly baby. Why waste all our time complaining? Don't you realize we have to wake up?"

She became suddenly quiet and afraid. "We won't go back, we'll refuse. Can't we escape now that we're together?"

"Come on back to the Big Pond," said 105. "Something was going to happen when you started babbling all that nonsense." They walked back together hand in hand to the Big Pond and sat down once more near the water. "Jim Gardner calls it mucky. Mummy says it's vulgar to say 'Mucky' but we use it in secret."

They watched the stirring weed expectantly. "Soon we shall know," said the little girl. "Now do you remember what you gave me?"

"Five Iron Nails, A Stick of Cinnamon and a Skein of Black Wool."

The water was parting. Two curved horns, then the head and neck of a black ram emerged. In its mouth hung a pair of golden scales.

The little girl drew a circle on the ground and filled it with different polygons, then pointing first to the left and then to the right, she exclaimed: "Fire and Air, you and I little brother; our mother is Earth and our father is Water. In twelve houses we lived, through twelve houses we will pass. When we hold hands across the circle, yours is Fire, mine is Air."

The black ram picked its way daintily out of the Big Pond and stood in the center of the circle.

The girl handed the boy a sharp triangular stone which he took in his left hand. Kneeling before the ram he caught its spiral horn in his right hand, twisting back its head and exposing the beating pulses of its neck. He cut its throat with the triangular stone. The girl caught the blood in her cupped hands, saying: "Drink the scarlet milk of Paradise, Little Brother, it is ours."

He bent his head and drank the blood out of her cupped hands. When he had also drunk he said: "The Old Gods are our food, the New Gods will be revealed to us in time and out of time. The Old Gods are dead; Earth, the Goat will renew the life blood of the Myth and will violate the Garden of Paradise. The Goat will deliver us the New Myth and she will be clothed with animal, vegetable and mineral; nothing dead, alive or unborn will she lack and nothing on this Earth or in the Nine Planets around will remain untouched by her or she by them."

The girl took the triangular stone and cut two meshes of wool from the head of the dead ram; one she entwined around the boy's neck, and the other she hid inside her nightdress. "This is a jewel and also a weapon: black wool rope into the center of the Earth where our roots were entwined at the beginning of life.

"Black wool, Black hair, Air roots for the night. Our roots into the Air, our roots into the Earth. We shall knit a ladder of Black hair and climb into the center of the Earth to our roots and when these long strands join again we will Hear, Taste, See, Smell and Touch."

They joined hands over the carcass of the ram and sang a song to the music of an old tune: "*Buj buj Zöldag Zöld*

Levelecske.... Open, Open little green leaf, Open, Open great stone door, You are the black ram, I am the black ram, it is dead so I am no longer I but you are I and I am you. Secret Enemy, we have quit the first house and have entered the fifth in the dark water."

"Water the place, we have met in Time."

When 105 awoke he was horrified to find that he had wet his bed. The dawn had already made the windows pallid and in an hour's time the waking bell would ring. He rolled around trying to dry the wet patch with the warmth of his body. Afterwards he would try and smooth out the telltale wrinkles in the sheet. They would find out, he thought, feeling his heart shrink to the size of a hazel nut. He would be humiliated and punished; they would make him sleep in the youngest children's dormitory, there would be no water for three days, everybody would know. Even humble 99 would despise him. They would whisper behind his back in class and in the Synagogue, he would be branded forever as the twelve-year-old boy who still wet his bed. He lay there miserably, imagining the consequences till the sharp peals of the morning bell brought him rudely out of bed and into the day's work.

The club-footed monitor preceded 105 up the strip of linoleum to his bed. He stopped suddenly with a clump of his shoe and indicated the damp wrinkled patch on the sheet. The bed was the only one not uncovered in the dormitory; 105 thought it looked white and guilty.

"What's that, Boy?" he asked still pointing at the patch of the sheet with a thick and rather dirty finger. 105 was dripping chilly sweat inside his striped coat but he looked the monitor in the eye and did not reply. "Well then, I'm speaking aren't I? Are you deaf? You've got a tongue in your head, speak up!"

105 remained silent and the monitor's voice started to

edge dangerously. "Come on Boy, I am asking you a question. I want you to explain just exactly what that is? Come along!"

Something in the persistent question suddenly stabbed 105 into a great rage. He felt the blood beating like a hammer behind his eyes. From without they looked like two hard black stones.

"I will give you five seconds to speak" said the monitor. He began to count out loud, still pointing at the patch on the sheet: "One, two, three, four... now one more chance... FIVE!" He grabbed 105's thin arm on the last word and slapped him hard on the face.

105 did not move. He stared straight in front of him with one side of his face red and the other white. The monitor released his arm and limped away: something in the boy's face frightened him.

Once alone, 105's teeth began to chatter and his body shook convulsively with dry sobs. When the tears began to fall he took refuge in the latrine. He let himself cry and rubbed his face on the grimy walls.

Far away in the building he heard the bell ring for morning lessons. Hurriedly dabbing cold water on his face to remove the tear stains, he ran to class, arriving a few seconds after the history master, who gave him an unpleasant stare.

"Well, number 105, so we've become a gentleman and arrive for class at the hour we please? I suppose one would say we are one of nature's gentlemen? Ha ha."

105 tried to shift into his seat beside the fat boy, 20, but the history master had not finished his little joke. "Take the chalk, boy, and write." He had already detected the signs of tears on 105's pale face. "And what do we see here?" His voice sounded damp and unctuous. "The gentleman of the class has been crying? At your age 105, I am surprised! At age

twelve tears are for females, or are we becoming girlish in our old age?"

One or two boys sniggered, but most of the class kept stolid cold faces. They hated the teacher and 105 was generally popular because he was brave and modest.

"Very well boy, take the chalk and write in even clear letters the exact date and description of the coronation of Szent Istvan."

When 105 turned towards the blackboard he had a clear picture of the date and circumstances of Istvan's coronation, but when the chalk touched the smooth black surface he drew a large perfect circle with a sweep of his left arm. The boys drew in their breath with a hiss but 105 went on drawing as if oblivious to everything apart from his strange occupation. He filled the circle with polygons placed in different positions. Their points touched the circumference of the circle in twelve places. The diagram was mathematically correct. He would not have said how long he had been drawing when the click of the opening door made him turn his head; he found himself face to face with the Director of the Institution. The wrinkled countenance behind the old man's long grey beard was impassive. They stared at each other for a long time.

"Zacharias," said the Director, "seems to have mistaken Szent Istvan's coronation for higher mathematical calculations. Zacharias, you have never shown an aptitude for mathematics up till now and the least I can say is that the time and place are ill chosen. Follow me."

105 wondered how he knew his name. Following the old man with some misgiving down the corridor, he turned over in his mind different plausible explanations for his exploit on the blackboard.

They entered the Director's study, which seemed luxurious and awesome to the twelve-year-old boy. True, the carpet was somewhat thin in places. Still it was a carpet and nearly covered the entire floor. Well-filled bookcases reached to the ceiling, giving the whole room a sober atmosphere which was not disagreeable. The ceiling was painted dark cream and had decorative molds in each of the four corners.

The Director made a sign indicating that 105 should take a chair while he sat himself behind a very large desk.

"Zacharias," he began, joining his fingers just under his large nose. "Reports lately on your behavior have been far from good; your teachers complain of a continuously rebellious attitude and a refusal to apply yourself to study. This cannot continue, Zacharias. Boys in your situation may not allow themselves the luxury of wasting their time. You are dependent on the State for your education and this is an eminently important factor for your future life. Moreover, remember that we are Jews and our lot is hazardous and difficult, not only in Hungary but unhappily in many parts of the world. Your life, like the lives of thousands of other Jews and gentiles, will not be easy. Lives are seldom easy, but a good foundation of knowledge is a strong weapon against the stones in the path of life; an aid in earning your bread— and let it be an honest bread!—and in preserving your dignity amongst your fellow men."

He paused and scrutinized the boy, who was impressed by the measured tones of his voice. They looked into each other's eyes with a certain understanding and mutual respect.

"Now Zacharias," continued the old man, "you are not a stupid boy, I might even say the contrary. But you are proud and willful, and these faults will be the source of great suffering when you take your place in the world. Pride is a form of blindness and therefore a kind of stupidity. The sage sees himself with such lucidity that the word 'Pride' ceases to have any meaning. He sees himself as a phenomenon amongst thousands of other mysteries great and small. A humble and dignified attitude is therefore the logical inheritance of his vision. A strong will is sometimes an asset in this life, Zacharias, but beware, for that element we call strength is often a mere assertion of a personality which blinds itself to reality and only seeks to obtain power and domination over its fellow men. Domination, Zacharias, is not only a great sin but is also a great waste of time because one becomes a slave of power, and life degenerates into a continuous struggle to maintain something which is no more than a conventional abstraction or word which men have made in a futile attempt to glorify their own ignorance and weakness. In learning the true nature of your faults you will have made the first step towards knowledge, and knowledge my child, is the doorstep of Paradise. Someday you will understand my words if you grow in the direction I suspect; you shall see what an immense and varied thing is real wisdom, how many and how strange are her faces. Never tire of seeking her, and do not despise her humble costumes."

He stopped speaking, apparently occupied with his own thoughts. The boy was embarrassed and pretended to find something on the toe of his boot. The old man took a piece of paper and made some diagrams, then he called 105 to his side.

"Can you tell me what this is, Zacharias?"

"Yes Sir, it is similar to the drawing I made on the blackboard in the history class."

"Quite so. Do you know what it signifies?"

Zacharias went red and hesitated before he replied: "No Sir, not exactly, Sir."

"But where did you learn such a thing?"

There was a long pause during which 105 shifted his weight from one foot to the other.

"I cannot say, Sir. I don't exactly know."

"Zacharias" said the Director sternly, "you must not lie to me."

"I cannot say, Sir."

The old man examined his face and finally told him to be seated.

"I believe you Zacharias, though it is most remarkable. Most remarkable."

He pulled his watch as the bell rang, ending the first lesson.

"You may retire now, my child, do not keep your teacher waiting. You may say that I detained you in my study. Go now Zacharias, we will continue this conversation at another opportunity."

105 saluted the Director and left the world of learning.

At eleven the boys were allowed ten minutes recreation before returning to their lessons. Black bread was served on a long wooden table in the school yard.

105 was no sooner outside than he was joined by 99, who wore a worried frown. "What happened, Zed?" he asked, taking his friend by the arm. "Did the Old Geezer jaw?"

"Not exactly," said 105, who was reluctant to disclose the details of the interview with the Director. "The usual stuff about work, behavior and manners. He was quite nice really."

"Quatch! You had guts to pull Dung Heap's leg like that! When you left he was shaking like a leaf."

105 gave a forced laugh. "Do him good the old stinker. He's had his knife into me the whole term."

"What was it?" asked 99. "It looked like some sort of geometry."

105 walked along whistling and throwing the five iron nails into the air and catching them again deftly. "Oh, something like that," he replied indifferently. "It just came into my head, any old thing."

"Well, it certainly made him waxy; better look out next time, he'll have you out if he can."

The bell summoned them back to class.

When night came, 105 waited in vain for the little girl and pony; perhaps his fear of repeating the previous night's accident kept her away. Many months passed during which he was obliged to evoke the Pink Lady to keep away dreams of the Inquisition and the scampering, moon-faced priests. The Pink Lady was still able to exorcise nightmares but she herself grew evasive and unreal. Her castle thinned to a flimsy structure like a painted theatrical backcloth. It had lost two of its dimensions.

105 passed the winter yearning; a yearning which became acute and anguished towards spring. He strove to ease his nostalgia by taking violent physical exercise and concentrating his affection upon 99.

The evenings grew longer and became warm. Sometimes the boys were permitted to take short excursions to the banks of the Danube where some of them bathed and others sat around inventing stories of drowned strangers and beautiful female suicides, stories of the Danube. . . .

During one of these excursions 105 and 99 discovered a huge orchard near the river. The exuberant display of half-ripe fruit tempted them. The orchard was guarded by vigilant keepers and wide dykes, but this only served to make the fruit more desirable to the two boys.

"Who could own such a big orchard?" asked 99. "And what a large family he must have to eat all that fruit."

105 was pensively eating the tender stalks of young grass. When he had them chewed to shreds he spat them as far as he could.

"It belongs to a Patriarch," he explained, "who has six wives and ten children to each wife. The only meat he gives them is cow's ears, and they eat the fruit so as not to starve to death."

"You're talking through your hat," said 99. "It belongs to a General who only eats meat and all that fruit is for the pigs. He has millions and trillions of jet black pigs."

105 spat a piece of chewed grass at least a yard. "Well I don't see why all that good fruit should go to the General's or to the Patriarch's wives. After all we're as good as pigs, or nearly as good because we're probably not edible after the food we've been absorbing for the past ten years.... Why not pay them a visit? A friendly visit of course, merely to leave our cards?"

"At night," said 99 excitedly. "We could muster a gang under oath...."

"Entire secrecy" replied 105, "is demanded; under pain of Chinese torture."

The expedition was arranged for the following night and was to include 19, 60 and 38 among others. The boys were to meet at the stroke of midnight in the school latrine and make their exit by the narrow window obscured by shrubbery and conveniently situated on the ground floor. Once outside the Institution they would take off their clothes and rub themselves with the grease 60 would obtain from the kitchen. Capture would be almost impossible, as anybody knows who has taken part in the greased-pig competition in a fair.

Each member of the expedition was to carry a small book-sack. Once in the orchard the boys would divide and obtain as much fruit as possible before the alarm was given, then each would save his skin as best he could. They were to meet again at the end of the drive, where their clothes would be hidden.

The latrine was to be the center for dividing spoils. Here 105 would supervise an even distribution of the stolen fruit.

Each detail of the plan was carefully examined and accepted, and on the following night the five boys went to bed in a state of high excitement.

A thin new moon was making her way across the dormitory window. Zacharias knew that when she reached the third pane midnight would strike and he would slip out to the school latrine. Thinking about it he realized that he did not really care for the fruit, but an hour's freedom in the night was as precious as a whole holiday.

The moon, slight and sharp as a knife, gave enough light for them to pick their way into the center of the orchard. They spread fanwise, each choosing a tree at different points of the compass. Their pale forms moved as quietly as shadows.

105 pushed his way through the long damp grass with his head bent and alert. Alone, he moved as surely as any nocturnal animal intent on his business. He stiffened to hear a foreign sound winding here and there, approaching him deviously. 105 crouched low and waited. In a short while he saw a small white object moving busily in the grass. On close inspection it proved to be a little dog which sprang towards him, wagging its tail and giving other signs of welcome and

recognition. The animal pranced about like a diminutive white horse cutting capers but when he bent to stroke it it danced away, waiting till he came near to prance off again. They played a circular game, drawing each time nearer to the oldest apple tree.

"Are you there at last?"

105 crept forward on his hands and knees; he saw somebody or something perched high in the branches of the oldest apple tree.

"Come quickly," it said, "I have been waiting so long amongst the tricks of time."

Afraid and excited, 105 started to climb the tree. Over his head crouched a young woman with long dark hair. She appeared not to see or hear him so he stayed still and listened to her voice, a bodiless sound that seemed to come from far away. Yet he heard it intimately in his ears.

"I need you now. Quetzalcoatl the serpent is sucking me dry. Wise King open the stone door, now I understand the black parrot's dying words. Man must open the door for I am impotent. Alone I am a pitiful and incomplete creature."

Looking down the young woman saw him. She spoke to herself: "Who is this? Is it the white child of Mesopotamia?"

He answered without knowing the source of his words.

"I am the white child, the wise King, the Jew, the Black Ram and the scales."

She stretched her hands out, willing: "I cannot touch you. We are separated by time. Let me in! Let me in!"

He cried out in anguish and tried to climb to her side but the twisted branches held him like a fish in a net. The young woman turned her face towards the moon and he saw that she was blindfolded.

"The Bohemian is surrounded by shadows. If my eyes

weren't covered I could read his past. The Bohemian was there when you were King on the frontier of Mesopotamia, the land where people are crockery. Mesopotamia faces Hungary across a mountain and a deep ravine, each spying on the other.

"Mesopotamia, huge arid cemetery, whose cities are tombs, whose trees are shaped lions and astrological artifacts. Holy, Holy Land, so holy that it is infested with prayers in the form of black butterflies swelling to the size of turkeys' eggs and forged with the life of the Mesopotamians; for seven decades their vitality has been sucked down the gullets of black butterflies. Even the wind is dead, leaving the prayer wheels motionless; the prayer wheels which once spun like tops. Facing this embalmed country across the mountain and ravine you lived, My Love, in a country of trees and snow.

"The stone door is closed against me, let me in, Oh my Love, let me in."

She shook the tree so violently that the fruit fell thumping to the earth in abundance.

105 lost his footing and fell amongst the apples. When he looked up the young woman had entirely disappeared. As he bent to pick up the fruit and fill his sack he heard somebody whistling in the distance, but the sound was so far and faint that he thought that it only existed in his mind's ear.

5

HE MADE a ragged dark figure against the snow-crusted street; haggard and dirty, his clothes jagged and torn, a mixture between a young scarecrow and the crows it was supposed to scare. The sole of his boot hung loose and the piece of newspaper inside soaked up the water and made a filthy pulp under his foot.

"My feet are so cold now I can't feel them anymore. So much the better, perhaps they'll drop off with frostbite."

"Zed! Zed!" He stopped at the sound of his name but did not turn.

"Zed!" Elias, number 99, caught him by the shoulder and looked deeply into his face. "Did you hear me call you?"

"Hello, El."

"Where have you been Zed? I've looked for you all over Budapest for months."

Zacharias smiled bitterly and started to walk as the cold slunk back under his clothes. "I came out of prison last week," he said. "There are so many jobs in Budapest I haven't been able to make up my mind."

El directed him into a café and they took a small table near the wall.

"Drink?"

"Offer me a bun and some coffee," said Zacharias. "Rubber dropped a pengő this morning on the stock exchange."

"Zed, you must tell me what happened. I might be able to help."

They ordered coffee and Szamorodni. El left a packet of cigarettes on the table: whole cigarettes, not damp butts picked out of the gutter and dried surreptitiously on the chestnut man's fire.

"Tell me all about it, you know I'm your friend, Zed."

"There's nothing to tell." Zacharias sipped his coffee, warming his fingers on the hot cup. "There's nothing to tell. I would much rather you tell me your own adventures; stories only make good telling once they've ended. My story hasn't begun yet. I'm still mere offal among the extinct ungulate mammals, waiting to learn slow movement. When the stone age begins—it seems to be a long way off—when it begins come back about my past. Till then I'll confine myself to asking for bread and insulting policemen."

El gave him a cigarette and sighed. "You haven't changed a great deal Zed. Still the same old petrified Zed so stuffed with humility and pride that he prefers to starve rather than ask for the help he needs.

"Never mind, if you prefer I'll tell you my own adventures.

"Old Aunt Sari died five months ago. With her went the pension. Having sold the little we had, paid for the funeral and the debts she left, I found myself on the street with five pengő in my pocket. A few hard and dirty jobs here and there, you know the type, then as luck would have it I was drunk one night in a café over by Hokay Ter and I got talking with a balmy Chinese. He wound up offering me a job and to my great astonishment the next day he remembered me and kept his word. I've been working for him ever since. He pays pretty well, he's not ever exigent and even if he is a bit cracked I'm thankful for his pay."

"What does he make? Sell? Steal? Cook? Grow or knit?" asked Zacharias, who felt revived by the hot coffee. "And where does he live?"

"Precisely near Hokay Ter, on a side street called O Ucca. The Chinese always seem to live on side streets, however wealthy they are. Perhaps because they're a secretive people, or we imagine them to be.

"In any case, this particular Chinaman is a queer case. He makes dolls, toys, music boxes, cheap paper fans and what not. He can make almost anything go with a sort of clockwork that he invented himself. There's nothing in the way of toy trains, soldiers, dolls that he can't make go in any way he pleases. He's a nice fellow though in his own way. I haven't quarreled with him yet, and on thinking it over I don't think I should like to."

"You are lucky," said Zacharias. "Employers are always swine; either that or insidious stinking dogs. There's no happy medium. I'd be content with just a slightly dirty swine, but they don't seem to exist."

"Well you don't have to starve. I have a small room in Lovag Ucca and earn enough to keep body and soul together. We will share and share alike. Remember the sour apples in the school latrine? What bellyaches we all had! It's funny to think we're the product of an orphan asylum."

"Yes I suppose we are," said Zacharias, "though I always thought of an asylum as a place where people gibber through iron bars with unkempt hair, wild eyes and long nails. I suppose our institution wasn't so far off…Twelve years locked up in a place like that is enough to give anyone a start in life. Quatch! What a start!"

"You remember the night don't you? Remember 'The General's' orchard?"

Zacharias suddenly became sad and silent. How empty his nights had been since he'd crouched in the oldest apple tree. He had tried to sift that painful hope out of his blood but it had clung to him through the years.

"Yes," he replied at last, "I remember very well. Are we supposed to forget just because we're what they call 'grown up'?"

"You will never grow up."

"I've had plenty of opportunity. Tell me El, have you got a girl?"

"No," said El. "No I haven't got a girl, and you?"

"Girls, yes I have girls when I have money. No money, no girl. There're not many who want to go to bed with a scarecrow. Not that I'm fastidious, but between hunger and a brothel I usually choose my stomach. It's not a question of principle but necessity. When the fat days come along again, I shall pick a nice blonde and put her in a bedsitting room which I shall visit at my will. I always had a fancy for plump blondes. There's lots to catch hold of and they wear well."

"Women are a poor use for our hard earned money," said El. "Give me a nice bottle of Szamorodni any day."

He paid the bill and they walked out into the street laughing. It was snowing again.

"Come to my place and I'll cook some supper. The bun you ate wasn't enough to fill a canary. I've become a good cook since my café days, you'll see."

Zacharias followed him with his bitter smile. The day was darkening and it was deadly cold; the snow capped his head and shoulders. Under the cold crown his raven's face was still and indifferent.

Chung Ming Lo used a basement in O Ucca as his workshop. During the winter days when the snow piled high outside a long twilight reigned in the shop, but at eight o'clock every evening Ming Lo pulled down the red blind to the disappointment of the children outside who loved to gather and spy on his workshop. Between six and eight however they could feast their eyes on piles of cheap toys, music boxes, wooden soldiers and a long carpenter's table furnished with saws, chisels, hammers, paint pots and sharp wheels spitting chips of wood.

Zacharias went to fetch his friend El at the workshop the evening after their encounter. He paused outside and peered in along with the children. He felt slightly guilty peeping into the workshop unseen. El was sitting at a side table painting half a dozen wooden trains bright red. A cigarette on the edge of the table sent up a thin line of smoke.

"If I lived alone on top of the highest tree in the world," thought Zacharias, "I could not be more outside the lives of human beings. Though if anyone ever asked me where I am, I doubt I could reply." He felt rather heroic, then depressed. It was cold.

"Let me in, let me in."

The nostalgia always returned monotonously when the sun went down.

"Won't you come in?"

Zacharias stiffened at the sudden words. Looking around, he saw the Chinaman at his elbow, a brick-red scarf wrapped around the lower part of his face.

"Come in," said the Chinaman. "I was expecting you. The cold is intense out there. It's not difficult to come in...."

"I'm a beggar," said Zacharias.

"Begging is a profession like any other, it takes a certain

skill. Even living is a form of commerce: we absorb the fruit of the Earth and pay energy back into the Earth. Work or art merely apes the natural order. You are a Jew, are you not?"

"Yes, I am a Jew."

"Then you understand me. That which is called forgetfulness in others is to a Jew a long shriek traversing his race from the beginning of Time. Among the Jews are those who can read the spoor of the road, hieroglyphs along the wayside containing the footprints and the knowledge of errant Jews. The Stars too can be read by man."

The Chinaman took a key out of his pocket and opened the door. Zacharias followed him after a short hesitation.

They were in a small poorly lit hall furnished with ornate furniture on fragile legs. Bric-a-brac clung to every possible space, leaving the walls invisible.

The Chinaman continued talking as he hung up his coat on a brass hook protruding from the jaws of a tiger.

"When a tiger kills his prey," he said, pointing to the hook, "he first tears out the liver and devours it. That liver is the best nourishment for the tiger. But how many other elements are contained in the body of an antelope?"

"Most enlightening," said Zacharias, who did not remove his coat, "but I should appreciate it if you offered me dinner rather than philosophy. Philosophy is an after-dinner game. Perhaps I am rude, but then I have nothing to lose if I never see you again."

"Frankly, if not altogether tactfully spoken," said the Chinaman. "Though you may gain more from me than you think. You will eat dinner here; we might interest each other. I am neither proud nor stupid, as you will see."

"Then you have my respect," replied Zacharias. "Real dignity cannot be affronted."

"You shall join your friend in my workshop," said the Chinaman, making for a curtain at the far end of the hall. "I am my own cook, slave and master. Please excuse me."

As the small man disappeared, Zacharias walked thoughtfully down the stairs to the workshop.

"Any luck?" asked El as Zacharias sat down on a wooden stool beside him.

"I haven't eaten since breakfast. There's no work, no hope of work. I'm cold and tired."

El looked up from his painting with a sly smile: "The Chinaman needs another assistant to catalogue the nick-nacks upstairs."

"He seems to like me," said Zacharias thoughtfully.

"I'm not surprised. He's a garrulous sort, and you did pretty well at school on the type of thing that amuses him."

"What type of thing amuses him?"

"Just talking."

"Well, I would sooner be paid for talking than for shoveling coal, washing dishes or doing arithmetic. We must fill our stomachs somehow. With our high class education I suppose it's best not to be too delicate."

"You're difficult to please," said El. "I took anything I could get."

"And what have I got?" asked Zacharias. "A cold in the head and an old suit of clothes."

"Look at my department upstairs." It was the Chinaman speaking. They did not know how long he had been standing in the doorway watching them.

"Upstairs I have toys for adults. Please follow me."

They mounted three flights of stairs and finally arrived in a dusty attic packed with junk or precious objects.

"Some I made myself," said the Chinaman holding a

candle aloft, "some are presents, and some are objects found or bought. Should you enter my employment it would be to catalogue and sort out the saleable items from the rubbish and to clean the former."

"You need only look at me to know that I need work," replied Zacharias. "But how do you know I'm honest?"

The Chinaman smiled: "Yes, I think you are honest, though my judgment could be in error." He lit an oil lamp. "Have a look around while I finish dinner. I shall be with you shortly."

When he was gone Zacharias crossed the room to a dusty convex mirror which hung on the opposite wall. Zacharias could not decide whether the mirror was black or so dirty that it appeared black. As he looked at his distorted reflection a sudden star-shaped crack burst in the center of the mirror where he had seen his face.

Frightened, Zacharias looked about for a place to hide the cracked mirror. On second thought, he realized that a gap on the wall would be even more conspicuous.

He turned away and hunted among the nearest nick-nacks for something to divert his thoughts. He found an old music box which was made in the form of a coach and four; he wound it up to see if it still worked.

"*Buj buj Zöldag*," sang the box in its creaky little voice. "*Zöld levelcske nyitva van az aranykapy. Kapuljatok rajta nyistd ki rozsam Kaputat kaputat hadd öleljem valadat, szita, szita peutek, szerelem csütörtok bab szerda....* Open little green leaf, Come in through the golden doors, For I miss the shoulders of my love. Wooden sieve, Friday, Thursday, green leaves, Wednesday, my love...."

The song has more words, thought Zacharias, yet try as he could he could not remember the second verse. Winding and rewinding the music box, he played "*Buj buj Zöldag*" a half dozen times. The thin tune evoked a nostalgic pain. He went back to stare at himself in the black mirror.

"You look like a scarecrow, I hate you. One cannot be astonished that such a jackdaw's face cracks mirrors. Ah, my soul and heart have withered up so small that both would not fit inside the skin of a fried bean. You are a particle in a senseless malady called life: a puzzle made by a lunatic, the winding circles lead to another puzzle sillier and more puzzling yet."

He turned around and felt foolish: Ming Lo had entered the room.

"He thinks I was admiring myself," thought Zacharias. "I wish I could feel happier."

"Strange what a puzzle one's own face is," said the Chinaman, who did not appear to notice the crack in the mirror. "How detached we are from our own faces."

"When I looked it cracked." After a rapid calculation Zacharias had decided that the truth would be prudent. "I am sorry, you will take it out of my wages."

"It is not a willful fault," said Ming Lo. "Perhaps you have been accustomed to see your reflection on another surface?"

"I don't think my face merits a great deal of attention."

"I wonder if you always thought so. Opinion is infectious when we are young, either high or low depending on the outside world's opinion."

"Perhaps one must be loved to love oneself."

"To be loved is a necessity while we drink our mother's milk. During adolescence when our virility is unformed we need to be admired, when that virility is formed but not satisfied, to hate. Later all these things fall into their right place, little tools hacking out one's form before our fellow men."

"As a matter of fact," said Zacharias, "I do not agree with you. Dreams, thoughts, love, virility and hate are too intimately entwined. To say one can exist without the other is like saying the perfume of roast coffee exists independently of the coffee."

"In which case," said Ming Lo, "you are destined to a great misery."

He took Zacharias by the arm and led him below; they were greeted with the pleasing odor of a roasting animal. At that moment Zacharias felt the kitchen was the most delightful place in the world.

On a sunless Wednesday morning Zacharias began to work in O Ucca. Furnished with a small black book and a pencil he set about sorting the varied, dust-ridden possessions of Ming Lo. While grovelling in an ornate tin trunk, he came upon a triangular box covered with black feathers fixed one upon the other as cunningly as if they grew on a bird. With some difficulty he opened the box and saw that it contained a stone key of Mexican workmanship.

Zacharias listened to the box which chanted: "Let me in, let me in. Open the stone door." He hid the box in his breast pocket.

Towards midday Ming Lo visited the attic, accompanied by a small man with a foreign accent.

"Monsieur Mangues," he explained, "is the secretary of Docteur le Fauvenoir, a French gentleman who is a collector. He wishes that you show him some objects of value which might interest the Docteur. You have not had a great deal of time yet to catalogue our possessions, but if you have happened upon any boxes, mirrors or keys please show them to Monsieur Mangues; Docteur le Fauvenoir is especially interested in keys."

Zacharias showed them a few small boxes he had found; they were in bronze, ebony or ivory, and of various origins. While Monsieur Mangues examined them, Zacharias could feel in his pocket the weight of the box and the stone key.

"You're sure that is all you have found?" asked Ming Lo. Zacharias nodded, without speaking. "There are nothing but empty boxes."

"I do have other objects which you could show to the Docteur," said Ming Lo. "Is he in Budapest?"

"Monsieur le Docteur is not in town at present," replied Mangues. "He is taking a rest cure in his country house. I am here on a small business transaction and intend to return to the country this evening. Whenever I visit town I have the habit of bringing a small present to the Docteur."

Ming Lo unlocked a mahogany cabinet and showed the Frenchman several objects in jade.

"You could take these pieces of jade to the Docteur. If they do not please him I will change them for something else."

When they had gone Zacharias went to the black mirror and smiled at his reflection.

"Locked doors" he said to his face in the black mirror, "are opened by keys. Stone door, stone key."

Towards seven o'clock the same evening Ming Lo joined Zacharias who was still sorting dusty treasures; he was holding a small package. "Stupidly I overlooked this this morning when Monsieur Mangues was here. It is a small ivory of ancient workmanship and I think it would please Docteur le Fauvenoir very much; I know he has no such piece in his collection. Would you be so good as to run out to Duna Palota Salloda and see if Monsieur Mangues has not already left? If he is still there give him this note and packet: I recommend this as entirely after the Docteur's taste."

When Zacharias was outside in the street he stopped under a lamp to read the note:

"The other is not presently in our possession; the enclosed is hermetically sealed, there is no cause to worry. Further particulars later. Do not be impatient, I shall join you within three weeks at Kentaur."

Zacharias broke open the seal on the packet and found a small ivory doll. It was obviously ancient. He wrapped the doll in its cloth and put it in his trouser pocket, then he walked about for a half hour whistling. He returned slowly to O Ucca and was surprised to find the Chinaman waiting in the street. "Well?" he asked with unusual impatience. "Was Monsieur Mangues at the Hotel?"

"He had left," said Zacharias. "The clerk said he had checked out at five o'clock."

Ming Lo considered this news in silence and finally shook his head. "That is very strange. I particularly wished Docteur le Fauvenoir to see that piece. I must ask you to do me a favor."

"What do you want?"

"I want you to take a small journey. I would like Docteur le Fauvenoir to receive the packet this evening. There is a train which goes as far as Pilisvörösvár, and from there you will find a sledge to the residence of the Docteur. The journey will take several hours and if you agree to leave this evening you could return tomorrow. The train leaves Budapest at 9:15."

Zacharias was pleased to oblige; a journey outside Budapest was always an adventure. So at 8:45 that evening he pulled his fur cap down over his ears and set out for the station with the packet carefully buttoned into his pocket. At 9:20 the train clanked painfully out of the station.

Zacharias shared a carriage with a man who wore a black

suit and dark glasses. He held a small leather book defensively before his face. His hands were pallid and unsteady. He must be a foreigner, thought Zacharias, because his clothes were cut in a narrow and unfamiliar manner. And how can he read through those spectacles? wondered Zacharias. A plain, elegant leather suitcase sat on the rack over the foreigner's head.

Something seemed to go wrong with the lighting in the compartment, and it became so dim that the white world moving outside was visible through the windows. The stranger lowered his book and looked outside. In the half light, the lower part of the man's face seemed to be featureless. Zacharias could not distinguish his mouth, even when he spoke in a mumbling, broken Hungarian.

"Do you mind if I open the window?" he asked. "The carriage is rather stuffy."

"He is English," thought Zacharias, rising and opening the window. "Where is his mouth...."

"Are you traveling in Hungary?" he asked, politely offering him a cigarette. If he takes it then I shall see, thought Zacharias.

The Englishman refused. "I never smoke, thank you. I suffer from chronic bronchitis. I find this climate very trying for the bronchial tubes."

"I believe you are an Englishman?" continued Zacharias. "You are visiting Hungary on a pleasure trip?"

"Yes, I am English. I am here not entirely for pleasure, but I am a great believer in mixing business with enjoyment."

"Are you going to Pilisvörösvár?"

"Thereabouts. They say it is a mining district."

"Are you interested in mining?" asked Zacharias, to make conversation. He still could not see an opening in the stranger's face.

"No, I can't say that I am. Old mines are of course interesting to me, as I am an archaeologist."

He handed Zacharias a neatly engraved card: "Peter Stone. Stonehenge."

"I am employed by the British Museum."

"I have never been out of Hungary," said Zacharias, "but I always wanted to travel. London, Paris, Madrid . . . they are like magic words to me. Someday I shall go to Paris."

"Well, do not miss the train. They say anybody who misses a love tryst or a journey to Paris dies without knowing they ever lived."

"I am sure that is true," said Zacharias. The train dived into a tunnel and above the clattering darkness he thought he heard the Englishman shout something.

"I beg your pardon?" said Zacharias, as the train clanked into the open night. "Did you say something?"

"I used to be frightened of tunnels," replied the Englishman. "When I was a child. They still have a disagreeable effect on my nerves."

"I was horribly frightened of the dark." Zacharias thought about his school days. "Frightened and fascinated. I saw things in the dark which were more terrible and more beautiful than anything I have ever known."

"Most children are frightened of the dark because they have a more acute vision than grown up people. Sometimes I think that a person who kept a child's sensibility as he aged would die of fright when the sun went down."

The wheels of the train squealed and drew to a noisy halt.

The Englishman let down the window and leaned out to see what had happened. Somebody was shouting.

"We're in a snow drift," he told Zacharias. "They are going

to shovel it away. We may be stuck for some time. What a nuisance. I was anxious to reach Pilisvörösvár this evening."

Five horsemen rode past the compartment window, looking into the train.

"Traveling in Hungary during winter is always rather hazardous," said Zacharias. "In England I suppose you don't get so much snow?"

"Fortunately we do not. A French poet once said: *'Pour ne pas que ça se perd, j'y vais vous dire mon opinion sur la neige: c'est de la merde qui fait sa première communion.'* I must admit I share his point of view. The only merit of snow is it is white."

The five horsemen returned and stopped at the window of their carriage. "Hey you!" called one of them. "Give us a cigarette." Zacharias tossed him what he had left in his packet. The man caught it deftly.

"Got a light too?"

"I wouldn't talk to them if I were you" mumbled the Englishman. "They might be bandits."

"What happened?" Zacharias asked the first horseman. "Are we snowed in?"

"Like a pig in a poke."

The Englishman was pulling at his arm trying to drag him away from the window. "Be careful, don't talk to them. You never know, they might be gypsies."

Zacharias shook him off impatiently and continued talking to the horsemen: "Will it be long?"

"It'll take them three hours or more. Maybe you'll see Pilisvörösvár by morning!" He let out a great hooting laugh and the horse tossed its shaggy head.

"If you let me get up and ride behind you I'd get there quicker."

"Jump up!" bellowed the horseman. "I'll give you a run for your money." One of the others had pulled a zither off his back and was plucking tunelessly on the strings.

"What did I say," hissed the Englishman. "Gypsies."

"Give us a tune" called Zacharias. "You with the zither." Five wild voices broke into song together: "*Buj, buj Zöldag Zöld*...levelcake....Let her in through the stone door. White Child. Wouldn't you kiss the shoulders of your love?"

"Come back! You can't do that!" yelled the Englishman, plucking at the disappearing tail of Zacharias' coat. But he had already landed unhurt on the snow. The horseman stretched out a dark hand and helped him mount. Whirling about, they took to the forest at a gallop.

"Fool!" screamed the Englishman in the distance. "The penalty for opening the door is...."

"Freedom!" yelled the horseman over his shoulder.

They lost the stopped train behind the trees and galloped along a winding track. Later they stopped to rest the horses and light a fire.

"My name is Calabas Kö," said the first horseman. "My four companions are Ivoar, Tej, Fa and Vas. They can only speak to music, otherwise they are dumb."

At these words the four men put out their tongues, which were cloven and colored like blackberries. The wagging black tongues made them look like cobras.

"Ivoar, play the zither," commanded Calabas Kö. "Tej, Fa and Vas, sing what you see."

"We see the sky, a spangled skin stretched dome-like over the world and her companions. The world is a fur ball. The moon is a nest of feathers."

"Enough Astronomy!" shrieked Calabas Kö, flinging snow

into Ivoar's impassive face. "They're always talking about astronomy. It makes me sick."

The four men dangled their dark tongues stupidly. Ivoar continued plucking at his zither.

"Calabas Kö," he sang, "you are an imbecile. Someday you will give up your soul like a belch of boiled cabbage. Your destiny is not even written in the sky."

"You'll pay for that!" screamed Calabas Kö, spitting in the singer's face. "I'd kill and roast him if the fire was big enough."

The four men in turn spat into the fire and started to sing once more.

"Hungary shares a frontier with Mesopotamia."

"There they go again," said Calabas Kö with disgust. "Geography."

But Zacharias leaned forward to catch each word they sang. "Leave them alone." To his surprise Calabas Kö held his peace.

"Hungary and Mesopotamia are divided by a deep ravine. Facing the desert you lived, my Love, in the mountains. Your palace on the highest peak in Hungary was surrounded by trees. Three kilometers from the Mesopotamian frontier. In your land the snow is your only cloak now, dear Love, but mine is my own wrinkled skin. *Buj buj Zöldag, Zöld Levelecski*, Open, open little green leaf, Open, open stone door."

Tej and Fa stood up and danced around the fire, clapping their hands to the rhythm of Ivoar's zither. When they had danced around three times, they sat down abruptly and Vas arose to his great height and sang alone in a penetrating treble voice: "Sweet Love, Dear Love, Eternal Love, listen to my rhyme, *Buj buj Zöldag, Zöld Levelecski*. Hungary's hairy men on their shaggy tiger-horses. Calabas Kö! Igen! Ivoar! Igen! Tej, Fa and Vas, Igen! Igen! Igen! Stone, ivory, milk, wood and iron but where My Love are Fire and Air?"

He sat down abruptly. Ivoar twanged his zither for a while before they started singing again: "White horse, red horse, black horse, Motion is the horse, there is no motion without the horse. The Moon is my love and my love is a horse. Five horsemen, Calabas Kö, Ivoar, Tej, Fa, Vas, who do you come to do homage?" Each man touched his lips, eyes, ears, nose and fingertips while his voice rose to a shrill treble: "We come for the Böles Kilary. To salute him we throw armfuls of glass on his path. The road is written with characters from the feet of errant Jews."

They threw pieces of glass into the fire and leapt to and fro over the flames without stopping their song: "His city is the forest. They burn whole fir trees for the Böles Kilary. But who lives in a bier covered with wolfskin? The Old Böles Kilary! Old Böles Kilary."

The five men circled round Zacharias and the fire, spinning together like a wheel. They called out like night birds: "Who are you? Who are you?"

"Zacharias, a Jew."

"No more?"

"I am Zacharias, a Jew."

"Then marry Fire for she is yours. Take her, take the Fire."

Zacharias bent over the blazing logs and stretched out his hands; the flames leapt up to meet his fingers and disappeared into his hands, leaving nothing but cinders and black charred wood on the ground.

Calabas Kö took a decagonal stone from his bosom and handed it to Zacharias singing: "Jew, this is your heritage from Solomon." Zacharias placed the stone in the pocket over his left breast. They mounted the horses again and took the road East.

They climbed a steep slope and the air grew rare and thin. The snow-ridden trees in the waning moonlight resembled script. Wolves' cries echoed over the steady beat of the horses' gallop.

Sweating, the five horses at last halted of their own accord before a solitary lighted tavern at a crossroads. As they dismounted Zacharias could hear a voice inside the tavern chanting, and the slow clapping of hands to the long wail of a mourner.

"Hey there, Janos!" yelled Calabas Kö. "Come out you limping spotted tyke!"

A man with a wooden leg hopped out of the tavern, his head and shoulders obscured by a black and scarlet hood. He addressed himself to Calabas Kö. "We have been waiting for three days, and the embalmers have not yet arrived."

"You stink like a corpse, Jancsi."

"I tell you the embalmers are three days late and Sari insists on keeping him warm with big fires...."

"Take the horses, feed and stable them, and get out of my sight."

Janos gathered the horses' reins without a word and led them around the corner of the tavern.

"You are the young Böles Kilary," said Calabas Kö placing his hand on the head of Zacharias. "Beyond a doubt."

When they opened the door a large black ram charged past them.

They entered a large kitchen lit by six candles. On a sexagonal bier lay the enormous corpse of a bearded king. The great recumbent body was clad in a long black shirt exquisitely embroidered with scarlet letters, circles, and polygons. His curling black beard reached as far as his feet.

The five men stood back as Zacharias walked slowly to the bier. He slapped his hands over his face: the dead king's features were identical to his own.

A red-headed woman who piled wood ceaselessly on the fire started to chant, keeping rhythm by striking the poker against the stone flags: "Böles Kilary, Böles Kilary, *Buj buj Zöldag, Zöld Levelecski*. Die Old Böles Kilary for the stone door cannot open till Young Böles Kilary lets you into the country of the Dead. Open, open little green leaf, for when you open the Earth must open too."

She peeped through her red hair at Zacharias with pale inquisitive eyes.

Calabas Kö and his four companions stepped forward and squatted around the corpse with closed eyes. The woman rose, took five red handkerchiefs out of the pocket of her skirt and blindfolded them. Then, sticking their fingers in their ears and spitting, they prophesied war.

"And when the massacre is done, the juice will germinate in the center of the Earth and split her crust and leap up on Land, in Water, in Fire and in Air. The old powers will seek to suppress it."

When they fell silent, the red-haired woman gave them warm water from a large jar, then wine from a stone jar and finally milk from an ivory goblet. Taking her place once more by the fire, she lit a pipe. As she puffed a thin music issued with the smoke.

Zacharias was so moved by this music that tears ran out of his eyes and with them went twenty years of bitterness. The red-haired woman watched him weep with a sly smile.

When she had stopped smoking the music she put the pipe in his hands: "It is yours," she said. "Use it well."

Zacharias put the singing pipe to his lips and blew but the only sound that came out was his own breath. The woman let out a peal of laughter. "Ah, no! You cannot use it to charm yourself! Young Böles Kilary, you must grow up! For you it has other uses."

She went back to the fire laughing and Zacharias, annoyed, hid the pipe in his pocket.

Having fed the flames with more pine logs, the woman walked over to the dead king and covered his closed eyes with her hands: "Böles Kilary, your old body must return amongst the dead. Your castle which was vomited out of the mountain will sink back from whence it came. The house of shadows: in the light between twilight and dawn, imprisoned in your castle, walk the bodiless shadows you loved and tamed. Remember your castle, Böles Kilary. Listen . . . constructed of black and red stones spat from the crater of live volcanoes through the Earth's shell. The stones were as huge as seven camels, three elephants and two horses squashed into a great cube.

"The stones that built your house contained old mineral knowledge from the nine planets. The walls of your house were wise, covered with presents, stolen objects and lost property. From the ceilings hung embalmed yaks from Tibet stuffed with preserved fruit, as well as Piñatas and country sausages. So many things hung from those ceilings, Böles Kilary! You could see all the animal, mineral and vegetable kingdoms in the universe looking up at your ceiling, Böles Kilary.

"Your furniture of precious woods, prehistoric bones,

mammoth's ivory and fur covered with lunatic drawings; the tables of turquoise glass with all the tints and reflections of the lake. Bouquets of Egyptian mummies stood like dry flowers in Syrian and Greek vases. Metals and jewels, heaps of jewels as high as the garbage dump outside the walls of Bagdad. This was your house Böles Kilary, Wise King.

"At night you combed your beard before nine trees burning in the grate, and you jumped a little when a wandering shadow tickled the nape of your neck. The shadows threaded softly through your hair, lost shadows....

"Coming and going from the hall were slaves laden with wine, rich cakes, milk, honey and succulent little birds. You gorged yourself, sometimes you threw whole cakes to your creatures. Animals sat in every corner and followed the slaves distractedly. Wolves and hyenas and exotic dogs from China, naked and no larger than a grown lizard; giant white poodles from France, with ears like huge rose-colored butterflies; dogs of every race and kind. Abundant cats and small black pigs, a mandrill and his female, three does and a stag, an Assyrian bull with a human head, owls as big as lions; ducks, turkeys and geese as fat as priests. All these creatures wandered near you because of your wisdom and tenderness.

"Sometimes you watched your beautiful face in a polished sheet of steel. You looked into your eyes for hours on end, Böles Kilary, but they said nothing. Still you talked to yourself: 'Gorgeous creature, Fascinating Wise King, Exquisite Jew, Savory body, what does she say, my lover, the Moon?' You laughed and your creatures gathered around you.

"One of those silent nights, when the snow fell outside, you looked deeply into your steel mirror and your image said: 'I hear.'

"Let me in, let me in, Stone Door."

The red-haired woman lifted her hands from the king's closed eyes and covered her own face.

"Böles Kilary, may these ten fingers suck up the perfume of your great wisdom."

A six-toned bell rang out; Janos limped through the kitchen to the door. They heard him call: "The embalmers have arrived!"

Everybody stood away from the corpse and the eight embalmers trooped into the room. Each bore a jar on his head containing sweet elixirs for preserving the dead; each man carried a Theodolite and a twig sprouting nine little green leaves. They wore masks and long yellow shirts girdled with swines' tails sewn into a rope.

The woman pointed over her head to the granary and the eight embalmers picked up the bier and followed her upstairs.

Calabas Kö and his companions let out a long sigh and lit their pipes. Zacharias sat down near the fire and fell into a reverie which eventually deepened into sleep.

Dawn had scarcely arrived when Zacharias was awakened by a black cat who rubbed itself against his ear.

Hearing sounds overhead, he guessed that the embalmers were still at work, though he had slept for several hours. The five horsemen snored soundly in their mantles. On the fire a pot of milk started to rise and froth. He leaned forward to pull it off the fire. No sooner had he moved than Sari ran down the stairs.

"He's hanging by the feet from the rafter," she told Zacharias. "He looks like a dead stag, his beard reaches the floor!"

She took the milk off the fire and scooped up a gobletful which she handed to the Jew. "Drink, little brother. The goat yielded a full bucket at three o'clock this morning."

"When will they be done?" asked Zacharias, drinking the milk gratefully. "Will it be long now?"

"They will have done at sunrise, when men are hanged. Listen young Böles Kilary. Millions of dead have passed through here and I have seen them lose their past and future. I would not have you do likewise. Now hear me, when the sun rises I shall call the eight embalmers down to the kitchen and feed them milk and bread. While they are still eating you must say to me: 'Sari, I hear a rat in the attic, let us hope he is not gnawing at the Wise King.' I will then reply: 'Why yes, I also hear something in the attic, take this broom and frighten it away.' Upon these words you will gather your cloak and run upstairs where you must cut down the Wise King and escape with him as fast as you can: the quickest way out is through the window."

"Very well," said Zacharias, "but where should I go?"

"If all is well a black ram will be waiting under the window; as soon as you jump he will take to his heels and you may follow him, for he was bred where you are going."

She wrapped up a piece of cake and gave it to Zacharias saying: "A piece of cake the mourners overlooked. How I cannot say, they nearly ate me out of house and home. Six geese and two sheep; seventy-five kegs of wine; most of them crawled home drunk as swatted cockroaches."

Suddenly she ran to the window and pulled aside the curtain. "Hey! The Sun is about to rise! Gather your wits Young Böles Kilary, soon you will have to set them loose again."

With her hands she formed a horn in front of her mouth and bellowed: "Come Master Embalmers, the Sun will be risen in an instant and I have prepared you milk and bread."

A few minutes later there was a shuffling overhead and

the eight embalmers came down the stairs. They brought with them a peculiar, sickly-sweet odor. Their long yellow shirts were stained. Without uttering a word they squatted on the floor in a rough circle and Sari served them mugs of milk and chunks of bread.

Calabas Kö stirred in his sleep and muttered: "Hyenas and tuberoses! Stinking beasts!"

"Sari," said Zacharias nervously, "I hear a rat in the attic, let us hope he is not gnawing at the Wise King."

She shook her head and replied: "Then take this broom and frighten it away."

Zacharias snatched the broom and his coat and ran upstairs stumbling. He found himself in a large granary. It had been tidied but still reeked of embalming fluids. The floor was stained and had been roughly swept. A great stone jar in the corner contained the King's entrails. Zacharias looked about for the King but all he could see was a small object, about the size of an otter, hanging from the ceiling. Looking closer he saw that it was indeed Böles Kilary, shrunken to the dimensions of a newborn babe. He took a stool and cut him down, then cradling him in his arms he climbed through the little window and leapt into the air. He almost landed on the woolly back of a black ram who, trumpeting with rage, galloped off down the road East.

Zacharias followed as swiftly as he could, holding the tiny bearded King in his arms like a baby. Zacharias soon found it less cumbersome to clutch the King by his beard and swing him in one hand, which, if not altogether respectful, was a good deal more practical and allowed him to run faster. He still held Sari's broom in his left hand, thinking it might be useful.

The twinkling black buttocks of the ram cut forked tracks

in the crusted snow ahead of him. The early morning was beautiful with a gaudy sky and the glittering white hide of the Earth.

Without looking at the country, Zacharias became conscious of the road rising; the forest had already thinned to an occasional tree. He seemed to be gaining the summit of a mountain. A hundred yards ahead the black ram disappeared around a bend in the road; when Zacharias got to that point the ram had disappeared but his tracks led up to a small plot of ground which seemed to dominate the whole world. The mountains rolled away to the sky; below, in a ravine between the two highest mountains, lay the Danube, frozen and still.

Zacharias looked around, recovering his breath. He let his eyes follow the course of the Danube, which seemed to eat a huge portal between the two mountains.

"The Danube emerges from a subterranean ocean," he said to himself.

He searched a while in the snow and finally found the ram's tracks which led downwards towards the ravine. He started off at a trot along the same course. The narrow, twisting path led down between trees and boulders. By dangling the Wise King from his fingers and using Sari's broom as a staff, Zacharias managed to descend swiftly without breaking his neck.

The mountains leaned over him as he descended to the Danube. The path threaded its way along the banks of the river to the gorge ahead but the tracks of the black ram ceased suddenly. Here the snow was beaten hard by the different footprints of man and beast; the tracks of claws, hooves and boots were entangled along the way. After gazing a while at his feet, Zacharias continued towards the opening in the rocks.

Far along the path he saw a huge man walking towards him. The creature was naked except for a black skin slung over his shoulders which dripped blood down his torso and legs to his feet. As he drew near Zacharias recognized the skin of a newly slain ram. The man's face was disfigured by a harelip. He had the pointed features of a dog.

"What-ho young man, where are you going?" The words whistled through his harelip. He had blocked the path with his huge body. Zacharias rapidly hid the Wise King under his cloak and held up Sari's broom like a weapon.

"Where are you going?"

"What's it to you, brother?"

"My business. Where are you going?"

"I am free to go where I wish."

"Free until something stops you," whistled the harelip giant. "I can stop you if I wish."

"How?" asked Zacharias, trying to edge past.

"Not so fast." He blocked the way. "If I skinned you I could have the pair of pants I lack."

Zacharias realized the giant meant what he said. "They would be too small," he suggested nervously. "Besides, I haven't any fur."

"True," said Harelip, "but leather suits me just as well."

"You need two cart-horses to make you a pair of pants. My skin wouldn't make you much more than a truss."

"There's no reason you should go on living. You're more useful as a truss, a pocket book, or even stuffed on my chimney place. So why should I let you live?"

"Several reasons," said Zacharias, thinking rapidly. "First, because in my own quaint way I like living; second, because I must find somebody before I die; and third, because even to you I am more use alive than dead."

"What use are you to me?" asked Harelip, "because that seems your only valid reason for living."

"With my hands I could make you trousers, sing you songs and cook you dinners more delicious than you ever tasted in your life. Also, I would bring you luck."

Harelip considered Zacharias for some time and eventually nodded his head several times. "Very well then, let us see if what you say is true."

"Hurry," said Zacharias, "if you want the pants by nightfall."

Harelip turned and led the way towards the portal in the mountains. Every now and then he looked back over his shoulder to make sure Zacharias was following.

As they drew near he could see through the gorge. Beyond the rocks Zacharias saw a frozen loch hemmed in on all sides by mountains; the light fell indirectly from the sky, which now seemed infinitely far away. In the distance on the opposite mountain he saw a castle.

Harelip stopped and pointed at the castle. "He's dead and they took him away," his voice whistled sadly. "But he will return."

On the near side of the gorge they came upon a construction resembling a cromlech. The low opening was covered with a sack which was frozen stiff. Harelip pulled this aside and, crawling in on his hands and knees, beckoned Zacharias to follow. The gloomy dwelling cut into the rock contained nothing but bones and rotted skins strewn about the floor. A heap of dirty straw in the corner evidently served the giant as a bed. The air in the cavern was heavy and fetid. Harelip collected some wood and, striking a flint with some dexterity, lit a fire in the middle of the floor.

"Now," he said, "I want my trousers."

"As you please," replied Zacharias, wondering desperately

how he would make a pair of trousers amongst so much garbage. "But remember that trousers are the first rung down the ladder of degeneration."

"I want a pair of pants," said Harelip firmly, "and if you cannot or will not produce them I shall have to make them myself, and you know how."

"All right," Zacharias fumbled, "but if I had such beautifully shaped legs as you I would not hide them under an ugly pair of trousers." He looked around the dwelling at the rotted skins and realized they were unfit to make clothes. Then the beard of Böles Kilary tickled his hand and a terrible idea came into his head. He remembered the dimensions of the King's body before it had been embalmed; if it had once been so large perhaps it could grow again. The least he could do was try. In its present condition however, he thought in despair, it would hardly cover the haunches of a decent-sized tom cat. He looked again at the expectant giant and decided he would try the experiment.

"Listen to me," said Zacharias. "I will make you a pair of trousers, but I must be alone for this and I shall need a cauldron full of snow. You must give me your word not to enter till I give you permission."

"How long will it take?" asked Harelip suspiciously. "You already promised they will be done by nightfall."

"Get me the cauldron full of snow and you will soon see," insisted Zacharias. "And bring another armful of wood."

The giant pulled a large iron pot out of a recess in the wall and carried it outside. He soon returned with a pot full of snow. Zacharias told him to set it on the fire.

"Now," said Zacharias, "get out and do not return till I call."

When the snow had turned to water and the steam began

to rise, Zacharias cut a thong of leather from his jacket and hung the Wise King over the pot.

"Humidity," he thought, "will make him swell."

The pot boiled and in the humidity and warmth of the steam the Wise King began to swell. Zacharias could hear Harelip stamping about outside. Like a plant growing before his eyes, the body of Böles Kilary filled the space above the pot. His nails and hair grew as rapidly as his body. Then with a sudden loud pop the Wise King burst: a cascade of spiced juices poured into the boiling pot. The Wise King's empty skin flapped huge and feeble over the fire.

"Now," thought Zacharias, "I can begin to make the trousers."

He took down the skin and with his pocket knife fashioned it into the rough form of a pair of trousers: cutting it in two at the waist and joining an arm and a leg as the trouser leg, the head and buttocks serving as the joining piece in the fork. He wove the King's beard into thread and, piercing holes with his knife in the skin, he sewed the pieces together into a creditable pair of pants.

Now and then Harelip called out: "Have you done yet? The sun is already low in the sky. Remember what you promised." And Zacharias replied: "They will be ready at nightfall. Be patient till the first star appears."

As the sun finally set Zacharias put the last stitch in Harelip's trousers and called out to the impatient giant: "Come in, Harelip, you have a pair of Royal breeches!"

Within a few seconds Harelip had entered the cavern and, grunting and swearing, wrapped his limbs in the Monarch's skin. He walked slowly around the cavern before making any remark, then he went up to Zacharias and embraced him, spraying him with fetid breath, and said: "You are my brother and my friend." Then, almost dipping his face into the boiling pot he exclaimed: "Ah, soup! And spiced like the King's own dinner!" He walloped Zacharias on the back: "You're a wizard, let us celebrate!"

Dipping a colossal mug into the mixture, he swallowed the boiling liquid at one gulp: "Delicious! Fit for a King! Help yourself my friend." Zacharias explained that he was not hungry and that he had already eaten. Harelip rapidly tossed off five mugs full of the embalming broth. Then, belching loudly, he sat himself down on the straw. Zacharias waited with interest to see the result of the giant's repast. He continued, however, in apparent health and even seemed disposed to talk: "Brother, you have shown yourself a superior creature. I surmise therefore that your mission must be of great importance, you are. . . ." He stopped suddenly and stared at Zacharias in sudden recognition. He covered his face with his hands and muttered: "It had to be. Salamander's double has returned among us."

"The Danube is born across the loch, isn't it?" asked Zacharias.

Harelip raised his head as if it bore a great weight. "That is correct; the subterranean ocean lies under the mountain Kecske. Beyond Kecske is Mesopotamia, the country of the Dead."

"Between Kecske and Mesopotamia, is there a stone door?"

"Yes," he replied heavily. "But the stone door only admits the dead into Mesopotamia."

"Just suppose," said Zacharias, "that a wanderer should wish to come out of the land of the dead to the land of the living through the stone door. . . ."

Harelip's great body trembled. "It would be disastrous; the Masters would never permit such a thing."

"I recognize no master," said Zacharias.

"That is what they wish. They govern without being recognized; nobody knows who they are. That is the secret of their great power."

"Do you know who they are Brother Harelip?"

The giant fingered his mouth, still viscous with the broth: "I know and I do not know."

"And where did you get such knowledge?"

"Across the loch, in the castle you can see from the doorway of my cavern, lived a Böles Kilary. This king was a prisoner because he escaped through the door, Kescke, from the dead. Those who return forget nothing, and so he was full of dangerous wisdom. The Masters set me to guard him; that was my work till he died."

"Once dead," said Zacharias cunningly, "they feared him no more?"

"Some say that when he passed through the door he was twice born. They still fear the Böles Kilary."

"And do the twice born possess the wisdom of memory?"

"They possess a half wisdom buried in dreams and omens."

"A whole could have two bodies," said Zacharias.

"The Masters would never permit that," answered Harelip. "They would arrange such a terrible fight between the two bodies that knowledge would always be obscured by hate. One would destroy the other, so only one half would be truly alive."

"These masters are powerful," said Zacharias. "Their power lies in the unit. The belief is one."

"You will be destroyed for knowing that."

"Why?"

"Because as long as a man thinks that he is whole in his one body he can never achieve the wisdom which would endanger the Plan. Believing that he is one keeps him in perpetual combat with another half of himself. Once he could see and accept that other half without combat, the Plan would totter like a ninepin."

"That," remarked Zacharias, "would not meet with the master's approval?"

"It would not be permitted."

"Why do you tell me all this?"

"Because you already know and because I know who you are."

"They why don't you kill me?"

Harelip stretched out his arms. As the ram's skin fell away Zacharias saw that he had many luminous moles on each arm which twinkled like a constellation.

"You are Air seeking Fire. To find her you must ride your Mother Earth over your Father, Water. The sacrifice of the ram is over; Ram must become woman and Air must become man. Then crossing hands in the center of the egg and alternately touching Fire and Air, their feet will be joined under Water."

So saying, he rose and went outside. Zacharias heard him playing a shepherd's pipe. This was followed by the bleating of a goat. At that moment a gust of cold night air blew the sacking away from the doorway; the fire reddened and sprang into flame, and Harelip stepped into the cave leading a white-bearded goat.

"She is the Earth, your Mother, and she is also a goat."

Harelip released the goat, which stood bleating and emitting white drops of milk from her full teats.

Zacharias knelt down and was suckled by the goat. When he had drunk his fill she started to walk around the fire in ever smaller circles, till her feet were in the flames. Then she threw back her head and screamed from the center of the fire.

"Time is," said Harelip. "You must cut her throat and drink her blood."

Zacharias took the decagonal stone, the gift of Calabas Kö, from his pocket and cut the exposed throat of the goat who offered no resistance. Then cupping his hands he caught the blood and drank it. Harelip pulled the dead goat out of the fire and flayed her with a knife shaped like a gnomon. He put the carcass whole in the cauldron and set it to boil.

"She will be your boat, Brother," he told Zacharias. "In her you will cross the subterranean ocean to Kescke, the stone door."

After some boiling the goat's flesh dropped off the bones. Harelip lifted the skeleton out of the broth and stretched the hide over it, forming a light boat.

"You must take to the water at moonrise," he told Zacharias. "Her skeleton is Saturn and will ride farther water at that hour."

Harelip then slowly stripped off his breeches and handed them to Zacharias, saying: "Brother, your boat must have a sail to catch the subterranean wind. Take my most prized possession and use them well."

They fixed Sari's broom as a mast and the skin of Ancient Böles Kilary as a sail. The little brig stood ready for her journey.

The moon rose. Harelip and Zacharias dragged the goat-ship through the gorge and onto the ice of the loch. They trudged toward Mount Kescke which loomed before them like a pale featureless head.

Harelip drew the small vessel behind him, the ram's skin

flapping around his shoulders and his great arms twinkling with luminous moles.

When they had almost reached the foot of Kescke, Zacharias saw the mouth of the cavern which led inside the mountain. The ice around the opening was hacked into chunks, creating a passage on the water.

"I shall wait till you return, Brother," said Harelip.

He pushed the boat off the brink of the ice and handed Zacharias aboard. The boat floated like a leaf. Taking a huge breath, Harelip blew powerfully into the skin of Böles Kilary. It billowed and the ship skimmed over the water and into the cavern.

Here darkness was different from night: it seemed full of the movement of water. Then as the boat penetrated further inside the mountain, subterranean bodies became luminous. Lights appeared around the goat-ship and slowly began to move before Zacharias. He saw the bodies shudder and shift; a sound moved through the mountain. It was the echo of a voice.

Somewhere in the recesses of the earth a light wind struggled free and tugged at the sail. The boat skid easily over the water with a soft lapping.

The echo freed other sounds; muffled shrieks and screeches, hoots and crashes followed upon one another. Light and sound bounced off the cavern walls.

The wind dropped as suddenly as it had started and the boat, after trailing a few yards slowly, lay still on the water.

Zacharias sat and waited. As time lengthened he began to worry, then worry turned into fear. The boat heaved slightly on the water. It was the only movement as the luminous bodies petrified around him.

The space around seemed square. To his panic, Zacharias

repeated over and over: "North, South, East, West. The four corners of the Earth."

The slight heaving of the boat became almost imperceptible, then it ceased altogether; the panic inside Zacharias became a hard solid knot. He thought he was hanging in eternity with no beginning or end, where life and movement no longer existed. He sat powerless and immobile with his panic, waiting for nothing.

A rigid and mortal battle was taking place amongst the subterranean forces: they were so finely matched that they did not move a hair's breath.

The scales quivered. Like a finger passing through a tree of hair, a gentle sound began in the head of Sari's broom; the gentle sound turned into a rustle and the rustle into a thread of smoke. Tiny sparks as small as insects' eyes appeared in the tuft of the broom and dropped into the water. Then little tongues of flame like agitated leaves on a tree: Sari's broom was on fire.

With a shriek Zacharias plucked the mast off the boat and dipped it into the water. It sizzled. He paddled forward, softly crying warm salt tears of release.

With the first movement of the boat light, darkness, and sound vibrated with a quality Zacharias had known but never seen.

The Earth itself seemed to yield up its own life.

He heard the roots of trees over his head suck their life from the minerals and putrid vegetation. He felt the struggle of death becoming life. He tasted acrid fear in the darkness. He smelt the stench of all beasts' desire. He saw all gradations of light, even those that vibrate in pitch darkness. And among all these things the voice continued calling: "Let me in!" It echoed a thousand times in the far recesses of the earth until it traced itself as a fossil in the stone.

Zacharias did not need to row anymore; the voice's magnetic power pulled the boat towards its source. He sat still, holding the broom on his knees.

They came in sight of a great stone door feebly lit by a large luminous egg hung lamp-like on a pole.

The goat-ship reached the edge of the subterranean ocean. It ground against a rough wharf hewn in the rock. It was made of jasperite and as red as blood. Zacharias leapt ashore and tied up the boat to an iron ring.

By the light of the luminous egg he searched for the keyhole. But he could find no keyhole, no opening of any kind in the smooth red face of the rock. The stone key hung impotent in his hand.

"I am here," he shouted. "We are only divided by the stone door." A long silence followed his words. Then with a sigh the voice replied: "Who are you? Have you come for me?"

"I have come out of snow, through the Earth and over the Water to find you. Our roots were linked before Time began. I am Air, the Scales. Who are you?"

"I am Woman, Fire and Ram. Where are you Dear Love?"

"I am in the mountain, Kescke, in the subterranean ocean which fills the Danube."

"I must be with you."

Zacharias searched the surface of the rock again but there was no keyhole.

"How can I open the door," he shouted, "when there is no keyhole?"

"Break through it with words, blows, prayers, or music. I've been waiting too long and it is breaking my heart."

These words were followed by a cry which ended in a bleat. Still holding the broom he thought of Sari and remembered the musical pipe and Ivoar's zither; the tune echoed through his head: "*Buj buj Zöldag, Zöld Levelecski*. Open, open little green leaf, Open, open great stone door."

He took the pipe from his breast pocket and put it to his lips. With the first breath the pipe uttered a long high shriek and burst along the stem into nine little green leaves. A great creaking, the sound of stone rending sent shivers into the marrow of the Earth. The goat-ship heaved and curled up like burning paper. Before his eyes a string of light opened; the stone door wheezed inwards as if pressed by a great weight. Then the air shuddered and vibrated with the bleating of five hundred white sheep which poured into the Earth like a deluge of curdled milk. Zacharias was swept aside by the stampede. He clutched a piece of rock which jutted out over his head.

The white flock took straight to the water and swam west. Zacharias recovered the goat-ship and hastened after the sheep, paddling swiftly with the broom.

A hot wind charged with dust, cinnamon and musk blew behind him from the country of the dead. The great stone door, Kescke, swung rumbling on the wind and closed with a crash.

Zacharias, rowing with all his might, followed the sheep west.

AFTERWORD

LEONORA Carrington's first novel, *The Stone Door*, was written in the mid-1940s, ostensibly to celebrate her recent marriage to her second husband, Emérico "Chiki" Weisz, in Mexico City in 1946. However, like her second, better-known novel, *The Hearing Trumpet*, *The Stone Door* was not published until the mid-1970s—first in a French translation in 1976 and subsequently in the original English in 1977. Perhaps this delayed publication is partly to blame for the fact that, compared to her visual production, Carrington's writing has been somewhat neglected and marginalized. Some of her early short stories, written in French in the middle to late 1930s, were published in France shortly after their composition (for example, "La maison de la peur," 1938, illustrated by Max Ernst, and the slim collection *La dame ovale*, 1939). Some of her short fiction written in English appeared in the American surrealist journal *VVV* and the literature and art magazine *View* in the early 1940s. *The Hearing Trumpet* was written in English in the 1950s, but was subsequently lost and not published until 1974 in a French translation. The English original was published in 1976. An English translation of *La dame ovale* appeared in 1975 and was followed in 1988 by the publication of two collections of stories, written mainly in the 1930s and '40s (and many of which were previously unpublished): *The House of Fear: Notes from Down*

Below and *The Seventh Horse and Other Tales*. *The House of Fear* includes *Down Below*, an account of the author's confinement in a mental asylum in Spain in the early 1940s.* This text was written in English, after which it was lost; it was then orally narrated by Carrington to Jeanne Mégnen in French. A portion of this oral account was translated back into English and published as "Down Below" in *VVV* in 1944. The entire text was published in English in 1972 and in French as *En bas* in 1973. This dizzying history of composition, translation, and publication may explain the relative lack of attention paid to Carrington's fiction: As Susan Rubin Suleiman has pointed out, Carrington "seemed to be caught between nationalities, between languages, between generations."

Possibly as a consequence of this complex history of publication, it is only Carrington's story "The Debutante" and the longer *The Hearing Trumpet* and *Down Below* that until recently have received substantial critical attention. Her most celebrated work is doubtless *The Hearing Trumpet*, which has been reissued multiple times (for example, in the Penguin Modern Classics series in 2005, with an introduction by the British novelist Ali Smith, and by NYRB Classics in 2021, with an afterword by the Nobel laureate Olga Tokarczuk), and hailed as a primary example of feminist proto-postmodern playfulness by several critics and scholars.

The Stone Door, by contrast, has remained a largely forgotten text in Carrington's oeuvre. Upon its publication in English in 1977, the novel received a lukewarm reception from critics. As for example the anonymous reviewer of *Kirkus Reviews* dismissingly wrote, *The Stone Door* is a "sur-

---

*Down Below was reissued in a stand-alone edition by NYRB Classics in 2017.

real fantasy of exasperating self-importance, only occasionally redeemed by a flash of wit or pungency.... Despite much portentous manipulation of lofty symbols, this is an extraordinarily vapid and tedious exercise." More recently, Tobias Carroll, in a review of Carrington's written oeuvre published two years after her death in 2011 on the website of *The Paris Review*, noted that "the disjointed narrative [of *The Stone Door*] renders this one of Carrington's less accessible works ... this is one of the few places where one of Carrington's narratives is unable to bear the weight of the accumulated history, myth, and philosophy in its allusions." Indeed, *The Stone Door* is a challenging text; even more than *The Hearing Trumpet* it repeatedly destabilizes its own framework by its many and sometimes overlapping layers. Moreover, its web of multiple narrative threads and perspectives and its convoluted esoteric symbolism sometimes obscure how the episodes of the novel hang together. The overarching thematic concern, though, is quite clear: All the different episodes or fragments in one way or another center around the discovery and opening of a stone door, which will result in the dissolution of the boundary between masculine and feminine.

The Stone Door is itself situated at a boundary, between two moments, two movements. Written as it was in the mid-1940s but not published until 1976 and 1977, it participates in the surrealist pursuit of a language and imagery freed of bourgeois repressions while gesturing towards ideas and concerns associated with the French feminism of the 1970s regarding the expression of desire and sexuality in non-phallocentric terms. We might say that Carrington's text anticipates this second cultural moment—but, because of the novel's late publication date, it also directly participates in it.

What we today refer to with the blanket term "French feminism" is of course a post facto (and no doubt reductive) construct. I use it here to refer to the writing of a group of theorists, such as Hélène Cixous, Julia Kristeva, and Luce Irigaray, that emerged in France around 1970, and whose members, in the words of Elaine Marks and Isabelle de Courtivron, were "convinced that there can be no revolution without the disruption of the symbolic order—bourgeois language, the language of the old humanisms with their belief in a coherent subject—and that only by dislocating syntax, playing with the signifier, punning outrageously and constantly can the old language and the old order be subverted." This search for a new language that pushes at the limits of the symbolic order is a through line between surrealism and 1970s feminism, and it is exemplified in Carrington's writing. Cixous's critique of phallocentrism and quest to renew language in particular chime with Carrington's concerns in *The Stone Door*. In her 1975 essay "Sorties," Cixous explains how "thought has always worked through opposition." Because of our patriarchal history, these oppositions, forming a "double braid ... throughout literature, philosophy, criticism, centuries of representation and reflection," are structured in a hierarchical relationship that privileges the masculine principle (or terms that are associated with masculinity, such as activity, culture, reason, Logos). The gendered bias of this relationship (which underpins both society and language in the symbolic order) is what Cixous calls phallocentrism.

Readers already familiar with Carrington's work will not be surprised that *The Stone Door* invokes a wide array of esoteric themes and symbols—from alchemy and the zodiac to Celtic myths and the Kabbalah. But I am not primarily concerned with tracing these allusions; rather I am interested in what the topography of the tapestry of references which structures the novel might communicate to us. I strongly believe that the significance of Carrington's writing (and visual art) exceeds the sum of its various esoteric references and intertexts. As Gabriel Weisz Carrington insightfully comments, "It is more fruitful to approach her work as a mythical imaginary construct all her own . . . a unique symbology." This view does not deny the potential Carrington found in alternative epistemologies—clearly she engaged with these with genuine interest—but it is conscious of their limits as interpretive frameworks. As Jonathan P. Eburne reminds us, "Carrington's art experiments in the medium comprised by the intertexts from which she draws . . . her aim, in other words, is not to follow hermetic or esoteric 'traditions' but to turn them, and the world they envision, upside down."

The Stone Door recounts the separate narratives of two characters (and their doubles and alter egos): a nameless woman in Mexico City and a young man, Zacharias, in (or outside of) Budapest. The novel circles around their pre-destined encounter, but up to the very end they meet only in dreams or daydreams. The protagonists are overtly associated with Leonora Carrington and her Hungarian-born husband, Chiki Weisz; several biographical details confirm this. For example, the female protagonist makes an appearance as a defiant six-year-old British girl, who, like Carrington herself, has three brothers, Gerard, Pat, and Bobby,* and a horse named Black Bess. Zacharias, like Weisz, is Jewish and

---

*Carrington's brothers were named Gerard, Patrick, and Arthur.

Hungarian.* Moreover, given that the novel is saturated with astrological imagery and symbols, it seems significant that the protagonists are associated with Aries (the goat) and Libra (the scales), since Carrington and Weisz were born, respectively, under these star signs.

The goal of both characters is to find and open a stone door, which will result in their union. At the same time as their intimated lovers' union at the end of the novel can be interpreted as a celebration of that of Carrington and Weisz, the protagonists also embody a feminine and a masculine element that together can be seen to make up a single individual subject. This theme is likely drawn from Carrington's extensive research into alchemy, a discourse that largely depends on dualisms (such as masculine/feminine) and their synthesis. However, rather than suggesting a platonic, ideal unity between masculinity and femininity—a synthesis that would erase the differences between them—the novel portrays the protagonists' union as an opening up and reconfiguration of fixed-gender identities and binary categorizations. This renegotiation is intimately tied to the novel's pursuit of a new creative language, beyond the confines of phallocentric structures. It is in the suggestion of a "bisexual" subjectivity (to borrow a term from Cixous), in which differences are preserved rather than eradicated, that the novel's most radical feminist potential lies.

Even though the plot of *The Stone Door* does not lend itself to easy summary, a brief outline of its narrative threads and episodes is important here, not only in order to extricate its thematic preoccupation with a new creative language and

*According to Susan L. Aberth, Weisz "suffered greatly during the Second World War, walking from Hungary across Europe to escape the Nazis."

gender articulation but also to illustrate how the very structure of the novel supports and enacts this thematic concern. The narrative opens "in the middle of a deep forest" where three men sit "silently in the observatory under the centaur... watching the moon which was well on the wane. They were dressed in clean white linen and sat at equal distances around a table. Each man had a telescope, a microscope and a flower which they examined meticulously, now and again jotting down a figure in chalk on the black table." This scene, which evokes motifs recurrent in Carrington's paintings, introduces what will later be referred to as "the plan": a seemingly all-masculine structure that determines how the universe operates, strictly guarded by two of the three men. The third man, referred to as "the Jew," however, is in rebellion against this patriarchal structure in favor of "a new chaotic order never before dreamed by man."

The second chapter introduces a new character, Amagoya, in a setting that appears to be Mexico City. For most of this chapter, Amagoya (who shares characteristics with Carrington, such as being haunted by a "legion of ancestral horses from the British Isles"), is absorbed in reading the diary of another unknown woman (who also bears a clear resemblance to the author), referred to only as "she"—a narrative thus embedded within the narrative of the chapter. Within this diary we descend several times into dreams, in which the woman finds herself in Mesopotamia, searching for "the wise King of all the Jews" as well as the "stone door of Kescke." The dreams themselves contain stories, multiplying the narrative frames and levels several times over. The chapter closes with Amagoya entering a dream state, transformed into a dog. There she meets the three men from the first chapter, who again quarrel over "the plan." The man referred to as the Jew (now identifiable as the wise King of the Jews from the diary) maintains: "The plan is stale and has been so now for many centuries. Only the mixture of male and female can make a living being."

The novel's third chapter focuses on two characters introduced briefly in the previous chapter—Phillip and Michelle. While they prepare a lamb stew, Phillip recounts a dream he had the previous night, in which he met a man without facial features. This man will return later in the real world of the novel, where he will reveal to Zacharias that he is a protector of the plan and employed by the British Museum. The fourth and fifth chapters focus on Zacharias, chronicling his childhood and adolescence in a strictly hierarchal educational institution. As he reaches adulthood, he gradually realizes that it is his quest to reinvent himself as the young Böles Kilary (Hungarian for "wise king"), the king that the diarist of chapter two met in a dream, and ultimately to open the stone door, which will destroy the plan and create a new order, uniting the masculine element with the feminine. On this mission, he is introduced to the dead body of old Böles Kilary, whose "features were identical to his own." He is persuaded to escape secretly with the embalmed body of the old Böles Kilary (now "shrunken to the dimensions of a newborn babe"), in order to return him to the country of the dead (where the female protagonist is imprisoned) via the stone door. What follows is an increasingly bizarre plot development, in which Zacharias encounters a giant, for whom he proposes to make a pair of trousers to avoid being eaten. Zacharias then proceeds to reinflate the body of the old Böles Kilary by suspending him over a pot of boiling water, subsequently stitching his skin into a pair of trousers. The novel ends with Zacharias sailing into the Mountain Kescke in a ship made of the carcass of a sacrificed goat (*kecske* is Hungarian for "goat"), with the Böles Kilary trousers for a sail.* There he unlocks the stone door with the help of a musical smoking pipe—a pipe that had originally been dug up from the ground in the dream of the diarist in chapter two.

As this brief sketch of *The Stone Door* shows, the narrative blurs or altogether dissolves the boundary between dream and waking life, and between reality and imagination. The structure of the novel offers no clear teleological line but rather resembles a Möbius strip, where the distinction between outside and inside has collapsed. The proliferation of these narrative layers and the permeability between them suggest something important about how Carrington attempted to reimagine language, gender, and subjectivity in this text. Whereas the novel invokes alchemical and other esoteric images that might seem to indicate a dualistic comprehension of gender and totalizing claims to knowledge, the nonlinear, fragmentary, and self-reflective form of the text on the contrary suggests a questioning of narrative and epistemological stability itself

Suleiman, in her perceptive analysis of *The Hearing Trumpet*, urges us to heed Carrington's experimentation with narrative form rather than engage in a literal interpretation of her esoteric symbolism. She argues that, in many feminist avante-garde works, "the framing is part of the content" and that this is particularly true for the way Carrington plays, in *The Hearing Trumpet*, with "narrative representation and

---

*This goat ship can be seen in the bottom left-hand corner of *Chiki, ton pays* (1947), which illustrates the cover of the present edition—a painting that in many ways reads like a visual companion piece to *The Stone Door*. In addition to containing many details symbolizing Carrington and Weisz's relationship, it features much of the alchemical and zodiacal imagery found in the novel.

framing—texts within texts, overlapping in curious ways." The way in which the narrative levels in *The Stone Door* enfold one another similarly undermines fixed interpretations of both the novel's own symbolism and the quest for a unified, "enlightened" self, which the alchemical journey might seem to be aimed towards.

The Stone Door and *The Hearing Trumpet* both employ multiple frame narratives and mise en abyme in order to challenge neat categorizations, whether they pertain to constructions of gender, subjectivity, or the separation between dream and reality. But whereas *The Hearing Trumpet* is parodic in tone, the same cannot be said of *The Stone Door*, despite occasional instances of Carrington's distinctive humor. Instead, it reads as her most probing, and perhaps also most earnest, fictional inquiry into alternative modes of representing subjectivity. Its experiments with narrative form suggest a critique of an understanding of the self as whole and unified, as well as of the symbolic order that traps the subject in a binary gender classification and identification.

The plan that the three masters are arguing over at the start of the novel is intimated to be nothing less than the perpetuation of patriarchy itself. The plan is powerful but it is also ultimately fragile—the novel makes it clear that it is the continued *belief* in its validity that gives it its power: "These masters are powerful," Zacharias tells the giant towards the end of the book: "Their power lies in the unit. The belief is one." "You will be destroyed for knowing that," the giant responds; "as long as a man thinks that he is whole in his one body he can never achieve the wisdom which would endanger the Plan. Believing that he is one keeps him in perpetual combat with another half of himself. Once he could see and accept that other half without combat, the

Plan would totter like a ninepin." Indeed, as one of the masters has already acknowledged: "If the omnipotent power fell into multiple hands [male and female], the working system would automatically disintegrate."

As indicated by the double focus of the telescope and the microscope in the opening scene of the novel, the plan structures not only the outer, social world, but also the inner, psychic universe of each subject.* Carrington is thus describing a system of male domination and female subordination upheld by institutions such as the Church, medical science, and Western philosophy, which not only shapes society but which has also been internalized by the individual subject. In true surrealist fashion, then, the novel calls for both a social revolution and a psychological one: We are reminded of André Breton's speech to the Paris Antifascist Congress in 1935, where he famously proclaimed: "'Transform the world,' Marx said; 'change life,' Rimbaud said. These two watchwords are one for us." In order to revolutionize stale conceptions of gender identity, Carrington suggests, we have to "unrepress" and create chaos where there is now apparent order, "and out of that chaos a new chaotic order never before dreamed by man" will arise.

One of the most charged and frequently used symbols in the novel is that of the goat/ram, which has multiple emblematic meanings, one of which is of course its linguistic connection with the stone door of Kescke itself. Associated with both the female and male protagonists, the ram, which is sacrificed three times in the novel, repeatedly evokes rebirth

---

*The combined foci are doubtless also an allusion to the esoteric axiom "As above, so below," which embodies the belief in the existence of correspondences between the macrocosm and microcosm.

and renewal. After the first sacrifice, Zacharias proclaims: "The Old Gods are dead; Earth, the Goat will renew the life blood of the Myth and will violate the Garden of Paradise. The Goat will deliver us the New Myth." The woman (at this point the six-year-old girl) proceeds to cut two tufts of wool from the dead animal—one for herself and one for Zacharias—and then responds: "This is a jewel and also a weapon: black wool rope into the center of the Earth where our roots were entwined at the beginning of life.... We shall knit a ladder of Black hair and climb into the center of the Earth to our roots and when these long strands join again we will Hear, Taste, See, Smell and Touch." Upon this, the two join hands and sing: "*Buj buj Zöldag Zöld Levelecske....* Open, Open little green leaf, Open, Open great stone door, You are the black ram, I am the black ram, it is dead so I am no longer I but you are I and I am you." As this passage makes clear, the ram is associated with the union and merging of the protagonists, of their sharing and inhabiting each other's identities. Such unity is in fact primary, it is suggested; masculine and feminine were "entwined at the beginning of life" and only split into separate spheres by socialization. The sacrifice of the ram stands for the undoing of this strictly dichotomizing and hierarchical categorization in favor of a mode of gender performance based on fluidity and multiplicity, which will result in renewed and expanded sensuality and desire ("Hear, Taste, See, Smell and Touch"). Opening the stone door itself—the separation between the two characters as well as the boundary between feminine and masculine—will result in a "sweet chaos" and a "New Myth." With the simultaneous association between the protagonists and the ram, on the one hand, and the ram and the stone door, on the other, the novel suggests that the line between what we define as masculine and feminine is discursive and located inside the psyche, that if these categories are unsettled, the human subject would open itself up to a richer and more expansive imagination and experience of desire. It also intimates that the Cartesian belief in a coherent, autonomous self is a limiting fiction. As Carrington would write in her 1970 essay "The Emancipation of Women" (also known as "What Is a Woman"): "I am that I am, God the Father told Moses on the Mountain. This means nothing to me. *I am* may have been a dishonest invention meaning multitude. / *Je pense donc je suis* [I think, therefore I am], but why? Some kind of pretension of Monsieur Descartes?"

Carrington's is a vision of gender and sexuality that resists binary thinking—of embracing difference without allowing it to serve a dividing or categorizing purpose. As such it resonates with Cixous's promotion of bisexuality as "the location within oneself of the presence of both sexes...the nonexclusion of difference or of a sex." In *The Stone Door*, the bisexuality inherent in each subject is suggested in the desires of the protagonists (and their multiple incarnations) to find the other (or others) within themselves and thus arrive at a kind of self-knowledge based not on a rejection of sexual difference but on multiplication and reinvention. Indeed, when on the last page Zacharias unlocks the door, he is not united with the female protagonist on the other side but instead overwhelmed by "five hundred white sheep which poured into the Earth like a deluge of curdled milk." The novel ends not with the anticipated synthesis between the two protagonists (or between masculinity and femininity) but with Zacharias frantically rowing after the enormous flock of sheep, which represents the multiplying otherness of the female protagonist. This deferred conclusion confirms

Carrington's view of subjectivity as bisexual, in Cixous's sense. The "presence of both sexes" within the subject "does not," in Cixous's words, "annihilate differences, but cheers them on, pursues them, adds more." If we open out to this fluid way of configuring gendered subjectivity, desire itself would be loosened from its current inflexibilities and cease to be inscribed by the "primacy of the phallus."

What Cixous refers to in "Sorties" as "the machinery... logocentrism...the great philosophical systems...the order of the world in general" is not all that dissimilar to the masters' plan in *The Stone Door*; it is the discursive mechanisms that articulate and rearticulate the social world as we know it in an endless process of repetition, which, in Judith Butler's famous phrase, "congeal over time to produce the appearance of substance." For Carrington, as for Cixous, language is at the core of both oppression and revolt; only by disrupting and subverting the old language can there be a "New Myth." This new language, which for Cixous is epitomized in what she calls *écriture féminine*, is inherently bisexual: "Writing is the passageway, the entrance, the exit, the dwelling place of the other in me—the other that I am and I am not, that I don't know how to be, but that I feel passing, that makes me live—that tears me apart, disturbs me, changes me, who?—a feminine one, a masculine one, some?—several, some unknown, which is indeed what gives me the desire to know and from which all life soars."

The first half of *The Stone Door*, which is mostly narrated by the nameless female protagonist, is particularly concerned with the problems and potentials of language. "Words are treacherous because they are incomplete," the woman proclaims. "The written word hangs in time like a lump of lead. Everything should move with the ages and the planets."

What is suggested here is that language, or the system by which we describe and understand the world around us, pretends wholeness and truth but is in fact an "incomplete" and hierarchizing human construct that has congealed or frozen into its fixed form; it is "stale," like the plan. This fossilized language is not just biased, it is also confining: "Hardly daring to touch what I want to say," the woman writes, "yet knowing that if I had enough space around me it would be a piercing shriek. White, long, sharp as the crack of a whip." This call, in what appears to be a new and more expansive (and perhaps bisexual) voice, invokes that of a red cardinal which appears earlier in the novel, able to fly through closed doors and windows. The cardinal had "a sharp voice, like a whip," which seems to allow it to break through the confines of the closed house. The proliferation of narrative levels in the novel can perhaps be seen to ward against a similar sense of claustrophobia within phallocentric language. The repeated acts of reframing seem to suggest an incessant attempt to get out of something, to find a speaking position outside a structure that is confining and oppressive.

The key to opening the stone door, and thus to the reimagining of gender, subjectivity, and language, is, as I indicated above, the music from a pipe. Importantly, in the novel, the pipe embodies multiple semantic meanings of the word: It is alternately and simultaneously a musical instrument and a tobacco pipe. This double meaning mirrors the many doublings and multiplications of characters, animals, objects, and symbols. The pipe appears for the first time when the unnamed woman diarist has just encountered the wise King in a dream and subsequently realized that "the bearded King was my mission." She meets the Egg, which has just hopped onto a painted tombstone (an allusion, perhaps, to Humpty-Dumpty and Lewis Carroll), and greets it with the words: "Our meeting must explain why I lost the black-bearded King. That I know." The diary entry continues:

> This produced no effect on the Egg so I realized that I must dive deeper to find the right words. When I could utter these words the reply would follow as fatally as day follows night.
>
> Taking a small trowel out of my sack I began to dig in the roadside for the word that would open the secret of the Egg. As I worked I repeated all the long words I knew such as federation, conspicuous, anthropology and metamorphosis. The Egg did not budge an inch. I tried one syllable words like am, art, it and off. The Egg trembled very slightly, without communicating any meaning to me. I then understood that the word to address such a primitive and embryonic body would have to come from a language buried at the back of time. The very moment that I understood this my trowel grated on a hard thing in the earth, and with a cry of joy I pulled a small pipe out of the ground. I put it to my lips and blew some notes which started low but mounted the scale rapidly till it reached such a high pitch that my ear could scarcely catch the thin sound.

This digging for words poignantly illustrates the search for a new language that can adequately express desire or knowledge outside the phallocentrically structured symbolic order. The novel indicates that there are no currently existing words that can name this "outside," but the new language takes the form of music, which perhaps signifies a form of expression that is more fluid and open-ended than the seemingly finite nature of individual words.

The music from the pipe is the key to the hatching of the Egg, out of which a White Child is born—a child who remains ungendered by the text. The Egg is an alchemical symbol, a hermetically sealed receptacle in which the substance (or the subject) goes through a symbolic death and is reborn as an elixir with magic powers—the philosopher's stone—which can change lead into gold or transform a person into an enlightened being. It is clear that Carrington is consciously invoking this alchemical imagery here, for the hermaphroditic child has also gone through a symbolic death: "Be fed by my death; I am half born but my death will be complete . . . my soul is the rope which hangs from the half circle of light into the half circle of darkness above and below the horizon." Like the philosopher's stone, the reborn White Child seems to be the catalyst for achieving enlightened knowledge, and following the child, the female protagonist knows "that our steps would go towards the person that I must find."

It would of course be possible to read this scene, as well as Carrington's novel as a whole, as an alchemical journey within the self—as an esoteric quest for wholeness and spiritual enlightenment. In alchemy, the hermaphrodite is the symbol of a union between the male and female substance. One could therefore interpret Carrington's experimentation with gender as an investment in alchemy as a path to spiritual wisdom. But it is equally possibly to read this imagery as a way of challenging the phallocentric language of the symbolic order. I choose to read her invocation of hermetic imagery and symbolism performatively, as a reaching for an alternative mode of expression that may have appeared to be outside phallocentric logic. In making alternative epistemologies visible, Carrington's work (like Cixous's) challenges and seeks to unsettle the monosexual and rationalistic discourse that structures the prevailing order. This is achieved not through advocating a new absolute discourse but rather through a seemingly irreverent and often humorous mixing of multiple mythic imageries. "Even at her most seemingly sincere," writes Eburne, "Carrington's tongue is always in her cheek; this ironic distance suspends the magical thinking of Carrington's use of esoterica and hermetic knowledges within an intertextual framework whose instabilities render it virtual rather than propositional." Indeed, the nonlinear, fragmentary, intertextual, and Möbius-like structure of Carrington's work undermines readings that attempt to lock the symbolic imagery into fixed and unified meanings.

In these ways, *The Stone Door* reimagines gender, sexuality, subjectivity, and, ultimately, language itself. This novel, because of the knotted process of composition and publication it underwent, historically belongs *both* to early postwar surrealism and to 1970s feminist avant-garde writing. Embodying a genealogy between these two moments, it adds a distinctly feminist contribution to the surrealist archive of attempts to artistically express the unconscious and its hidden desires. At the same time, it anticipates what Marks and Courtivron in the 1980s would call "one of the major questions facing feminist and nonfeminist thinkers today": the pursuit of a speaking position that is not complicit with phallocentric ideology and that can accommodate difference and otherness. As such, *The Stone Door* deserves to be reconsidered as one of the most important visions and revisions of gender, sexuality, and subjectivity of the surrealist movement.

—ANNA WATZ